THE CRUELEST MONTHS

THE CRUELEST MONTHS

Dorothy K. Fletcher

To order additional copies of this book, contact:
Xlibris Corporation
1-888-795-4274
www.Xlibris.com
Orders@Xlibris.com
15521

CONTENTS

Acknowledgements 9
Prologue 11

SEPTEMBER

Lesson 1 17
Lesson 2 29
Lesson 3 37
Lesson 4 43
Lesson 5 49

OCTOBER

Lesson 6 57
Lesson 7 61
Lesson 8 68
Lesson 9 72

NOVEMBER

Lesson 10 79
Lesson 11 83
Lesson 12 89
Lesson 13 93
Lesson 14 97
Lesson 15 102

DECEMBER

Lesson 16 109
Lesson 17 113
Lesson 18 117

JANUARY

Lesson 19 125
Lesson 20 130
Lesson 21 134
Lesson 22 139
Lesson 23 143

FEBRUARY

Lesson 24 151
Lesson 25 157
Lesson 26 162
Lesson 27 169

MARCH

Lesson 28 177
Lesson 29 182
Lesson 30 187
Lesson 31 191
Lesson 32 195

APRIL

Lesson 33 201
Lesson 34 204
Lesson 35 210
Lesson 36 217
Lesson 37 222
Lesson 38 226

MAY

Lesson 39 231
Lesson 40 237
Lesson 41 241

JUNE

Lesson 42 249
Lesson 43 253
Endnotes 257

For my mother, my best and most important teacher.

ACKNOWLEDGEMENTS

My sincerest thanks go to all those who have given so freely of their time and their love in the completion of this work—Hardy Fletcher, my husband and great love of my life; Emily Carmain, my editor and Fernandina friend; Eve Lucken, my friend and spritual supporter; Jean Cosby, my teaching colleague and great adviser; Byron Riggan, my uncle and most gentle writing mentor; and all the thousands of students who have endured my many classes and enlightened me as I have taught.

PROLOGUE

As Lydia and I slowly helped Mr. Smythe down the dark hall toward the office, I could feel him trembling down through his arm that I gently cradled in mine.

"You're going to be just fine, Geoffrey," Lydia said to him softly. "It's all right, honey. You're going to be just fine."

All I could think to do was pat the arm that I held.

Mr. Smythe stared straight ahead, as if we were leading him to his execution. His eyes brimmed with tears, and his mouth kept saying something I couldn't quite hear. Eventually, I realized that he was repeating the same thing over and over. "I'm not well. I'm not well."

Of course, both Lydia and I could tell that he was far from "well."

Just a few minutes before, as we headed toward the faculty lounge to get Cokes for our planning period, we had passed his opened classroom and found him talking with great animation to the air. Thirty-five empty desks faced him as he explained the relationship of Ahab in *Moby Dick* to "modern man's relationship to megalithic governmental structures."

For about a minute he was unaware of our presence.

"Geoffrey, what are you doing?" Lydia finally asked.

"I beg your pardon?" he said, turning stiffly to face us.

"What's going on?"

"I don't understand." He adjusted the bent wire-framed glasses that were sliding down his nose. He was perspiring profusely as if it were 95 degrees in there.

"I'm teaching my class," he said, pulling himself to his complete height.

"Geoffrey, you're talking to an empty room," Lydia said.

With unsteady legs, he lowered himself into a chair.

"I was afraid this was going to happen," he said, resting his head in one of his shaking hands. Chalk dusted both of his palms. "You see, I've just been so afraid of these children that one day I began pretending that they weren't there—that the seats were just empty space and that their comments and taunts couldn't hurt me anymore."

As his words began to sink into my consciousness, I relived my own pain at the hands of teenagers. After all, I had been teaching for less than a year and already I had often been overwhelmed by the sheer terror a roomful of adolescents could produce in me. I suddenly could see myself in Mr. Smythe's place—worn down by years of abuse from teenagers.

"For a while," he continued, "my plan worked. I could keep doing this job simply by imagining the little monsters gone. They just weren't going to make me hate this career. I wasn't going to give it up. Their tyrannies disappeared when I willed them all away, and I was left here to do what I loved most without any fear or pain."

"Geoffrey," Lydia said gently as she moved over toward the broken man.

He kept talking. "But it wasn't long, though, before I realized I couldn't tell the difference anymore—whether there were any people out there or not. The room appeared to be empty, always. It's been empty for three weeks now. I think. I mean, I'm not sure at all what's happening."

"I'm so sorry, Geoffrey," Lydia said as she gave him a comforting hug. "Let's get you home, okay?"

Carefully, we took the dazed man to the office where his son would be called and they would go home. As the three of us made the slow, sad journey down the hall, I wondered if this were where I too was headed; if at the twilight of my career, I would have to "imagine" my students into oblivion so that I could stand my existence. Only time and many hard lessons would tell.

SEPTEMBER

LESSON 1

April is the cruelest month.

The Waste Land
T. S. Eliot

Some say that April is the cruelest month, but those of us who teach know that it's actually September. The quiet days of college are gone, when our biggest worries were staying awake in the last few methods classes and keeping our GPA's from slipping. That easy part of life is gone forever, and most sadly, the glorious mornings of June, July, and August no longer stretch before us like a warm, sunny beach running endlessly to the horizon.

My cruelest September came in 1990, the September after I had graduated from Florida State University with a Bachelor of Arts in English and a 3.24 GPA. I had dressed in my best navy blue suit and armed myself with teaching certificate and carefully prepared plan books. Then I drove the seventeen miles from my garage apartment to Paul Lawrence Dunbar Senior High School, an inner-city school on the north edge of Jacksonville, Florida. This ultramodern edifice, a one-story, blonde brick building with a flat roof and very few windows, loomed before me that morning in a large field. This was the site of my first teaching assignment, and the beginning of a lifelong career in teaching, I hoped.

As I parked my car and prepared to disembark, I felt so nervous that I became light headed and thought I might faint. My heart pounded violently, and I could feel a cold sweat spread slowly over my body. The night before, I had convinced myself and my new husband, Michael, that I was ready to face the call of education. After all, I had interned in a really tough school—Wakulla County Senior High, near Sopchoppy, Florida. That high school was the only one in the whole county, and most of the children I taught there were the kids of either big, burly farmers or thick-armed, slow-speaking fishermen.

These crude and uncultured "rednecks" were a real challenge to teach. Sopchoppy was hardly a cultural oasis. Here, cheerleading and baton-twirling were still high art forms and the boys were far more interested in "fixin'" their cars than in "fixin'" their grammar. For the most part, however, we were of the same race and culture. There was still an unspoken kinship between us, and our lives had many similar points of reference. The situation at Paul Lawrence Dunbar was going to be very different, and I guess that difference was what had me panicked this September morning.

As I locked the door to my car, I could see multitudes of well-dressed, brown-skinned students gathering at the entrances. Some listened to music on Walkman radios. Others danced or swayed to the sound of booming car radios that vibrated deeply as low-riding, souped-up cars rolled slowly past the school. Other kids were chasing each other in friendly games of tag. Most of the students were talking excitedly, using hands and flashing bright smiles. It didn't look too terribly menacing.

Suddenly, a wave of nausea swept over me as I moved toward the building. It was all I could do to pass through the crowd that I felt sure was gawking at me. I made it through the front door of the building and rushed to the women's faculty restroom as fast as

I could move my short little legs. There in the sanctity of a narrow bathroom stall and without any dignity at all, I lost all the breakfast that I had been able to choke down that morning.

When I finally emerged spent, shaken and weak-kneed, a kind-faced, gray-haired black woman approached me. She wore a blue linen dress and appropriate gold accessories.

"Oh, my God! You are the whitest white girl I have ever seen. Are you all right, honey?"

"Uh, . . . I've just been . . . terribly ill, and . . ."

"Let's get you out of here so you can sit down. You look terrible. I don't want you fallin' out on us in here."

She took my arm to lead me out, and I wondered how I would ever make it through the day. As we moved slowly toward the faculty lounge, I could feel the unsettling nausea being replaced by a rising flood of tears. There were maybe ten minutes before the bell would ring, and hordes of teenagers—angry, white-society-oppressed, black teenagers—would be unleashed upon the school and me. Somehow I had to compose myself or all would be lost from the outset.

"You're going to do just fine," my new friend said to me as if she could read my thoughts. We walked slowly down a quiet hall.

"Of course," I said to her; to myself.

We entered the faculty lounge where about five other teachers were already sitting, drinking their coffee or finishing the last of their lessons for the day. The helpful woman assisted me into a chair at the large table in the center of the room. I closed my eyes and breathed deeply as my yoga instructor had taught me way back in my freshman year of college. In through one nostril, out through the other. In. Out. In. Out. Soon I was centered and only mildly terrified.

"Try not to let them see you smile," the woman said, gently. I opened my eyes and realized she was getting me some Coke from a bottle she had in the small refrigerator. Carefully, she poured the liquid into an old, battered coffee mug.

"Here," she offered, and I gratefully took the cup from her

hand. Her friendly face lifted my spirits considerably, but I still felt puzzled by her first remark.

"For the first three months, dear, don't let them see you smile. It makes them think you're on their level. You know what I mean? You don't want them thinking that. You want to keep it strictly business. Save your smiles for after Christmas."

"I'll remember that," I said gratefully to this wonderful person. I took a small sip of the soothing Coke and, thankfully, held it down. "I'm Donna Webster, by the way, a new teacher in the English Department." I offered my hand.

"I'm Lydia Morrison from math," she said, as she gripped my hand firmly. "You think you'll be all right now?"

"No, but I'll try," I said, laughing just a little.

"Well, just holler if you need any help. Someone is sure to come."

"Thank you," I whispered.

Lydia patted me on the hand she still held and gave me another warm smile. I closed my eyes again and did not watch her leave. I coasted in semi-consciousness for another minute, maybe two, then resigned myself to my fate. I gathered up my things. I wanted to get to my classroom before the bell rang so I would not be overwhelmed by a tide of humanity when the bell signaled the start of the day.

I made it all the way to my room—Room 409—while the halls were still empty. I was really very lucky. Unlike my other F.S.U. friends who were fortunate enough to get teaching jobs in Florida, I was blessed with my own room. My buddies had to "travel," which means each of their classes was taught in a different room. I didn't have to do that. At Dunbar, the enrollment was low and getting lower as the suburb schools syphoned off students faster than we could attract them. This meant our classes would be large, but each teacher had his or her own space. I, for one, was elated.

During the planning days that preceded the start of school, I had scrubbed clean and decorated with posters and plants my own newly painted haven. I had posters of London and Stonehenge and all manner of pithy sayings on all the walls. I had put a small fichus tree in the corner near the only window, a couple of aloe plants in a corner, a cactus dish on my desk, and several variegated plants with their tendrils draped over the corners of each cabinet.

I walked into this clean, well-organized place on that first day, hoping to find it as I had left it on the afternoon before. When the lights went on, I sighed. Some of my posters had slid off the wall and were lying in crumpled heaps upon the floor. I silently cursed the masking tape that some veteran teacher had warned me wouldn't hold up much of anything. Then I set about getting the place in order before the first student entered the room. The bell rang before I could even step, and I knew then this was going to be one of those days.

I hurriedly picked up the posters and shoved them into a closet to deal with at a later time. Then, I rushed to the door to greet the students as we had been instructed to do in our introductory faculty meeting. Students had begun to pour into the halls by the hundreds, all of them sporting their new fall clothes, shoes, and book bags. Automatically, I smiled at the first face that made eye contact with me. I remembered what Ms. Morrison had told me about no smiling until after Christmas; but when that student's brown face returned my smile with a warm grin, I filed Ms. Morrison's advice away in the back of my head. I didn't stop smiling at students for the rest of the day.

My first official task was supervising Homeroom 911, a group of wildly energetic freshmen who were composed of mostly the D, E and F last names. These children were also as new to this school as I was, so we had at least that one thing in common.

When the bell rang, I was pleased to see that each student had taken a seat and gotten quiet. Fear, I surmised, was what made them so agreeable. I got right down to the business.

"Good morning, everyone. My name is Ms. Donna Webster . . ."

"You're not married?" a cute little girl at the front asked.

"Actually, I am married . . ."

"But you said 'Miss.'"

"Well, I actually said 'Ms.' which is supposed to be the same as 'Mister.' You know, you can't tell whether a man is married or not by his title."

"Don't you want people to know you are married?" a different child asked.

I wondered what my liberated friends would say in answer to this question. I was glad they weren't there to judge my performance. "No, that's not it," I stumbled. "It's just that it shouldn't matter whether I am married or not as to how well I teach, does it?"

"You got any kids?" someone in the back asked.

"Not yet, but . . ."

"How old are you?" a young man at the right side of the room asked.

I paused for a moment to catch my breath. I didn't want to let it out that this was my first year teaching, so I skirted the issue entirely by saying, "I am old enough to know when people are trying to get me off track. So enough about me. We have a lot that we must do this morning."

I went to my overhead projector, upon which I had placed a prepared transparency containing detailed instructions telling the students what we were to do in homeroom that day. I flipped the switch to turn the machine on, when a dull popping sound told me at once that the bulb inside had just blown. It would take at least 15 minutes for me to locate and procure another bulb or projector, so I simply would have to use a more ancient and time-honored way to impart information. I could have used the chalkboard, but I had no chalk since I am allergic to it and hadn't planned on using any. I had planned on preventing sneezing fits by using the electronic technology we had so readily available. Silently, I now cursed that technology. I was getting yet another lesson in adaptability. I finally had to fall back on probably the most ancient form of educational communication—the voice.

Following my transparency agenda, which I now held in my

hand, I began by calling the roll. The task proved to be one of the biggest challenges of my life. Unlike my ancestors, who named their children after kings and queens of Europe—John, Mary, George—I understood already that many black people create the names of their children using sound as a measure. This was especially true of the girls' names—Shondria, Tawanda, Vermeshia, Chelseia—names that if said properly can fall like music on the ear. I really liked the idea of naming children in that fashion, but at the moment, I was bumbling my way through the list.

"Rhodeshia?"

"That's Rhodezzzzia!"

"Rhodezia? Rhodezia. Sorry about that."

"Humph."

Next on the agenda after roll call came the issuing-of-schedules. I handed the first one to a student, and no sooner had I moved to the other side of the room to give out a few more than the first student began to call out my name.

"Miss Webster, how come I got first period gym? My mama came up here last year and told them I shouldn't have gym at all."

"Hey, me too, Ms. Webster," the second student said, "only I told them I didn't want algebra."

"Yeah, Mrs. Webster," called the third, rising from his seat, "I already passed Spanish 1 this summer. I got to go see a counselor."

"Wait a minute now!" I said firmly, stopping in my tracks and holding out my arms as if to stem a great rush of people. "Just everybody take a seat! No one goes to see a counselor today! Understand? Counselors are too busy working with the brand new students."

"Well, I'm as important as any new student," one of the front row girls informed me.

"I know you are, but all you'd end up doing is sitting in the office the rest of today. You can at least get some things accomplished if you stay here and do things my way. Besides, they told us to keep you all in the rooms until after homeroom, okay?"

Reason seemed to prevail, at least for the moment. I finished giving out all schedules, and then began to give out pieces of paper from the mountain of forms that needed to be filled out. I handed out the emergency consent forms, the I-have-seen-the-Code-of-Conduct forms, the Federal Assistance Program forms, the Free-and-Reduced-Lunch forms, Health and Accident Insurance applications, and finally the Student Locator form. When there was only the locator form left for the students to fill out, the bell rang to announce the end of homeroom. I was horrified.

To myself, I said, "This cannot be! How could even a seasoned, veteran teacher complete all the tasks required in such a short time?"

"What do we do now?" one confused little freshman asked with imploring eyes. "What do we do?"

"Uh, just give me all of your forms, and I'll fill them out for you the best I can. Now, just go on to your next class."

A mob of children surrounded my desk as they brought up their papers, and I tried futilely to get the forms into appropriate piles. I gave up finally, because at least five children were surrounding me asking how to get to their next classroom. I had to quickly analyze the map I'd mounted on the wall near my desk so I could tell them how and where to go. While I was doing this, my first class of juniors was rushing in, and my door was unmanned.

"Ms. Webster," a stern adult voice said over the din and confusion. "Why are you not at your post?"

I looked over to see the unsmiling, leather brown face of my principal, Mr. Ward, at my door.

"Oh, I'm sorry," I said, warm embarrassment spreading over my face and the unsettling feeling of nausea rising in my stomach once again.

As I moved toward the door, so did the little clutch of ninth graders who were each demanding my attention. I felt like a mother bird with her chicks clamoring about her for food. Mr. Ward said nothing more and moved on to the next class to reprimand the teacher who wasn't at her post either.

The bell rang while I was still imparting my last set of directions to my last ninth grader.

"Will I get into trouble for being late?" she asked in a panicky sounding voice.

"Not on the first day, darling. Just tell your next teacher you are new to the school, and that your homeroom teacher is new to the school as well. I'm sure they will understand your tardiness."

I closed my door, turned to face my classroom and beheld at least 40 bodies in there, maybe more. Some students had to stand since I had only 35 desks. I had to think fast. I gave my chair to the nearest student and the two table chairs I gave to two more. Then I sent two students next door to see if we could borrow any desks, and they were sent back empty-handed. In violation of every rule I knew, I allowed the remaining two boys to sit on the rectangular table I'd placed against the back wall.

I took a deep breath. "My name is Mrs. Webster, and this class is eleventh grade standard English. Please check your schedules now to be sure you are in the right place."

There was a scuffling sound as the students consulted their schedules. Then, when no one left the room, I proceeded to call the roll carefully so I'd make only minimal mistakes in pronunciation.

"Carolina?"

"That's Caroleena."

"Sorry."

"Humph."

When I got through the roll call, I was able to actually teach a little. Since my overhead was dead, I was thankful that I had thought to Xerox a handout of class rules and procedures.

This I went over orally before I issued the first novel that the class had to read—*The Bell Jar* by Sylvia Plath. There were numerous groans and sighs from the audience, and I did a remarkable job of ignoring it, as I gave out the relatively tattered paperbacks.

"Your first assignment is to read chapter one and be ready for a quiz on it tomorrow."

"You have got to be kidding," one huge young man at the back of the room said. "It's just the first day of school. Why do you want to load us up with assignments already?"

I opened my mouth to speak, when the young woman named Carolina spoke for me.

"This is a high school class, Harold, remember? It's a lot harder in high school than it is in middle school. Besides, this isn't like the other remedial classes you're in."

Laughter spread quickly throughout the room.

"I know this is high school," Harold said back to her, "which is why I am surprised you're here."

"Oooo!" the rest of the class said in unison.

"Besides," he continued, "I just don't think it's right to have to start the first day off with an assignment. I mean, I want to get to know the other members of the class." As he said this, he leaned over toward the young woman next to him and put his arm around her shoulders.

"Uh, . . . remember me?" I asked politely, raising my hand as if I were a student myself. A slight ripple of laughter made its way up to me. "Assignments are really not open for debate. If you have a problem with anything in this class, you may see me after school or call me at home at this number—372-1689."

A few of the students appeared to have actually written the number down. When I looked up, I encountered a room filled with shocked faces—mouths open and eyes wide.

"You're giving us your telephone number?" Carolina asked.

"Yes."

"Your HOME telephone number?"

"Yes. Why?"

"No reason," she said, shaking her head.

Just about that time, the bell unexpectedly rang to signal the end of Period 1. That was when I remembered that each class had been shortened to accommodate homeroom. This "class timing thing" was going to take some getting used to.

As the students rushed out, I hurried to my station at the

door. Of course, the principal was nowhere to be seen to observe me doing a good job.

"Oh, well," I thought. "So it goes."

The rest of my classes were as crowded as my first class and as confusing as homeroom. I had been assigned five classes and three preparations. First period was eleventh-grade standard, which covered American literature. Second period was eleventh-grade honors, covering American literature at an advanced level. Fourth period was regular senior English, which was mostly British literature. Fifth period was another eleventh-grade standard class. And, I had another standard senior English class during the last period of the day.

That day, each class provided me with many stimulating challenges. There were the trial-by-roll-call, the rules-and-procedures ordeal, and the why-do-we-have-to-start-working-on-the-first-day-of-school debate. By my last class, I had thankfully sidestepped every obstacle that had been thrown my way. As the children piled out of my room at the final bell and I began straightening up my desecrated desk, I silently congratulated myself on not throwing up, in public at least. I had, however, considered doing so after I had eaten some stale vending-machine crackers during my third-period break, but I held fast. I also congratulated myself for not falling apart or crying at any of a number of things. I had actually survived my first day of real teaching. All I had to do now was prepare myself for the next day. I still had to collate all my homeroom forms that I also had to complete. I had to rehang my posters. Then I had to reread the first chapter of *The Bell Jar* for both 11 standard classes, the first chapter of *The Scarlet Letter* for the 11 honors, and the first installment of *Beowulf* for the senior classes. I then had to prepare and type up the lessons and quizzes that went with the readings, since I wasn't at all sure I could rely on the overhead any more. I figured I had at least four hours of work ahead of me, and I was absolutely bone tired.

I would go home and nap for three hours. I would then stay up until 1:30 a.m. to have everything ready for my second day of teaching, and I would awaken at 4:45 a.m. so that I could make it to school by 7:00 that next day. With luck, I would make it all the way through the day without losing my breakfast. With luck, I would again survive all that an educational system can throw at a person, and I only had 179 more days of this to go.

LESSON 2

The grisly sea-beasts again and again
Beset me sore; but I served them home
With my faithful blade as well-befitting.

Beowulf

It was an amazing discovery to me that the mascot for Paul Lawrence Dunbar Senior High School was a Viking. Somehow the vicious ancestor of the modern day Anglo-Saxon had no business representing inner-city children, most of whom were the descendants of Nigerian tribesmen and warriors. A warrior of some Watusi tribe would seem to be a more appropriate representative; maybe a soldier from an Ethiopian kingdom would better stir the hearts of these students than would some Viking warlord. But I am not the one in control of the world, and it was the community that chose this symbol as the mascot for its children. No matter how incongruous the Viking mascot seemed to me, no one was going to change the symbol that had represented this school for over thirty years.

At any rate, I thought if I were able to tie the school mascot to

Beowulf, my seniors would have a ready-made point of reference to help them understand this ancient, sometimes-hard-to-follow character in their textbook.

"Now, I want all of you to close your eyes and imagine what I tell you."

"Is she for real?" I heard Avery, a massive hulk of a person, ask his neighbor.

"Flesh and bone real," I said. "Now, close your eyes, Avery, and do what I ask."

"He's afraid of the dark, Ms. Webster," Roscoe, a mahogany-dark skinny kid, said from the other side of the room. Everyone laughed.

"All right, class. Let's settle down. Now, I want you to close your eyes and imagine Arnold Schwarzenegger as Conan, the Barbarian."

"Who?"

"What?"

"Never mind. Let's start over. Imagine Arnold Schwarzenegger as the Terminator."

"Okay, we see him," Avery said. "Now what?"

"Well, imagine this same muscular guy in a bear skin."

"Oooeee, Mrs. Webster! Does your husband know you do this?" Roscoe asked. More laughter.

"Ha. Ha. Ha," I said coldly. "Now, do you see in your mind the guy I am describing? Armor, shield, sword."

"Yes . . ."

"Good. Then you know exactly what Beowulf looked like. He's tremendously large. And he is so strong he can swim in the ocean in a full suit of armor. For days. Can you see the sweat rolling down his face?"

"Can you smell it?" Mario, one of several Puerto Rican students, asked.

"Mario, cut it out!" I warned, my eyes still closed. "Can't you see the bulging muscles? Can't you almost feel his animal-like power? He's a super hero, like Superman or . . ."

"Wrestle mania?" Roscoe asked.

"Well, I guess so. A Jesse Ventura type. Yeah. That's good, Roscoe. Actually, Beowulf looked a lot like our Viking mascot. Okay. Now, you all may open your eyes."

I held up a drawing of our mascot which had been drawn on a football program I had borrowed from one of the coaches.

"See. Beowulf probably looked like this. He probably had wild red or blonde hair under a iron and leather helmet. His face would have a great bushy beard. He might have an animal skin tunic, and he probably hadn't bathed but once or twice in his life."

"Ew!" the class said in unison.

"He is certainly not a person to tease or harass. Why, when Grendel the monster starts eating Beowulf's men for a midnight snack, Beowulf simply rips the monster's arm off with his bare hands."

"Ew!"

"Neat!"

"Yeah!"

"Then, he takes that arm and drapes it over one of the rafters for everyone to see and to scare off any other monsters that might come along."

"You are kidding, aren't you?" Marvelette, a large-busted, big-hipped woman/child, asked.

"Well, not very much," I assured them, "but I still think you'll love this story. It is every bit as scary and action-packed as any TV show or movie you can imagine."

"Scream I, II and III?" asked Mario.

"Oh, at least as scary as that. Certainly as bloody."

"What about women?" Mario continued.

"What about them?"

"Well, are there any honeys in the story?"

"There's the queen, Wealhtheow, but she keeps her skins on the entire story."

"Aw," the class groaned.

"Okay, then class, let's open our books to page 35. Who will read first from the adventures of Beowulf?"

Percy, the Beowulf-sized quarterback for the Viking football team, slowly, almost carefully, raised his hand. He had been sitting quietly in the back of the class all the while I had been talking. I had liked Percy from the moment he sauntered into my classroom. His skin was soft and smooth like a warm cup of hot cocoa, and he had shaved his entire head in solidarity with the football team. His shoulders were massive, and his 6-foot 4-inch frame dwarfed my 5-foot 2-inch height. I had to throw my head back to look him in the face. It was worth the effort, though, because Percy's smile was pleasing, and his sparkling eyes made me want to smile right back.

"All right, Percy!" I said, almost joyously. I had been afraid I would have to wait forever for volunteers.

"Mrs. Webster?" he asked. "Did this really happen? I mean, were there really Vikings and monsters and all?"

"There really were Vikings. They lived in the Northern areas of Europe like Norway, Finland, Denmark and Sweden. As for monsters? I don't know. I bet there were some pretty frightening creatures back in the old days, but I don't know if you'd call them monsters like those in the movies today. What do others of you think?"

There was a bit of mumbling that went around the room.

"I think this stuff is all a bunch of bullshit," a girl named Tamara said.

Tamara would eventually become one of the most negative forces I had ever and would ever encounter in my life. She proved to me that just one person strategically placed in a classroom can make a teacher's life a living hell. Tamara, who had a tall, imposing figure, would soon begin to confront me about assignments and why did they have to do what I said anyway. She then would refuse to do the work I assigned and would go "ballistic" whenever she had a failing average, which was often. She would talk incessantly and make fun of my clothes, my hair, and my speech. She would mock my speaking voice by repeating everything I said in an unflattering, nasal tone. No matter what I said, Tamara would find a way to twist it into something other than what I had intended it to be. I would always thank God whenever Tamara was absent.

During my first encounter with her, the class had fallen silent, probably wondering what my reaction to her breach in classroom decorum would be.

"Tamara, I am glad you have strong opinions," I started.

"It's TaMARa," she corrected curtly, using the unflattering, mock-teacher voice I would come to hate.

"I'm sorry, TaMARa," I said carefully as a hot blush spread over my face, "but I'll thank you to keep the profanity to yourself from now on."

"I didn't use profanity," she said forcefully. "You'll know when I use profanity."

"I'm sure," I said, feeling anger continuing to rise within me. "Why do you not approve of Beowulf, TaMARa?"

"Because he's white, and I'm sick of reading stuff about white people."

"Well, I hate to tell you this, but in the twelfth grade the state of Florida says we should study British literature, and there will be a disproportionate number of white authors we must read. That is just the way it is."

"See? What did I tell you all?" Tamara said as she turned to face the other members of the class.

"What did you tell them, TaMARa?" I asked.

"I told them that I knew you were the type to find excuses for everything. You're just like all white teachers here at this school."

"Is that supposed to be an insult?" I asked.

"Maybe."

"Well," I said slowly, trying not to lose my temper, "I guess I act like a white teacher because I AM a white teacher."

There was a brief and awkward silence, my mind racing the whole time trying to find a way to hold on to my authority without looking like I might suddenly fly out of control.

"You know," I said at long last, "TaMARa, I think that you may have a point about the unevenness of the curriculum. I will make everyone in this class a deal. If someone can find an alternative black character—a hero like Beowulf, only African—then I'd be willing to share the story with the class and make a study of that character as well."

"You know we can't do that," she snarled angrily. "We'll never be able to find a person like that."

"I bet if you did a little research, you could find one. The library here has a mountain of African tales and stories in which you could find appropriate African heroes. As a matter of fact, I think this could turn into a great project. Who would like to go to the library and see if there are other more appropriate heroes for black children?"

I waited an appropriate amount of time, while two, then three hands went up to volunteer. Tamara's hand was not among them.

"I'll give major extra credit for anyone who finds me a good character," I bribed.

"I could do that," Percy said, his hand joining the other volunteers.

"There you go again, Percy," Tamara said with a hateful and venomous voice. "Always sucking up to the stupid white teachers in this school."

He didn't even flinch. He just sat there as a big grin spread across his face. "Mrs. Webster, you'll just have to excuse Tamara. She has a real bad attitude against humanity in general."

The bulk of the class laughed nervously, and I half expected some sort of explosion to come from the girl. She apparently thought better of continuing her attack on one of the school's most respected and popular students, because she turned back to me and calmly said, "You know we ain't going to find nothin' worth reading about because the white people who write the books don't give a shit about representing black heroes in a true fashion."

"TaMARa, no one has even gone to the library yet. How can you even know that only white people are the writers of the books with African heroes?"

"It's just the way it is in a white-run society. The whites control everything we see and hear and watch on TV. They control what we read in books and what we are forced to learn in school. Then, they send drugs in here to our neighborhoods and enslave the black people all over again and they don't even need no chains."

"What are you talking about?" I finally asked.

"I'm talking about the truth, which you apparently don't want to hear." Tamara smugly crossed her arms across her chest and dared me with her posture to say another word.

"All I want to hear right now is the sound of Percy's wonderful voice reading the lines of Beowulf starting on page 35." I tried to speak as liltingly as my furious voice would let me. It wasn't easy.

Percy finally began to read the story, which he did exceedingly well. His deep voice rose and fell appropriately, and he gave the story an air of excitement. He read dramatically, sometimes using his arms, and his enthusiasm carried over to the next reader, who continued the narrative with spirit. I occasionally had to stop the flow of the story to explain characters or vocabulary words that the students did not know, but the whole exercise began to be rather enjoyable. I could almost imagine a bunch of Geats sitting around a mead hall fireplace with a roaring fire and hanging on every word of their "scop," or storyteller. Almost.

Tamara had put her head down on her desk when Percy first started his reading. Soon she was sound asleep, missing the reading and the rest of the lesson.

When the bell rang, she was the first out of the door. Others took their time to collect their books and lunch bags to go to the next class. As I straightened my desk in preparation for my next class, I soon realized that Percy was looming over me. Looking down upon me, he put his hand on my shoulder and said, "Don't you let Tamara get to you, Mrs. Webster. She's just got a problem with white people. It ain't nothing personal against you. I've seen her start stuff with every white teacher we've ever had together. She's even run a few off, but I don't want her to do that to you. Okay? You just pay her no attention, and I'll always be here to help you out if you need it."

I swallowed hard, hoping he would not notice the tears welling up in my eyes at his kindness. "It will take more than a Grendel-like TaMARa to run me off," I said with mock bravery.

Percy smiled at my little joke and then moved majestically toward the door.

"See you later. Just remember what I said."

"I will, Percy. And thanks."

LESSON 3

That man over there says that women need to be helped into carriages, and lifted over ditches, and to have the best place everywhere. Nobody ever helps me into carriages, or over mudpuddles, or gives me any best place! And ain't I a woman?

Look at me! Look at my arm! I have ploughed and planted, and gathered into barns, and no man could head me! And ain't I a woman? I could work as much and eat as much as a man—when I could get it—and bear the lash as well! And ain't I a woman? I have borne thirteen children, and seen them most all sold off to slavery, and when I cried out in my mother's grief, none but Jesus heard me! And ain't I a woman?

"Ain't I a Woman?"
Sojourner Truth

If ever anger were personified in one human being, then it would have been embodied in the form of Rochelle in my Standard 11 class. Her entire being screamed at me. It was as hideous as she could make it. Her hair had not known the comb or pick in weeks and strands of it poked out at wild angles from her head. Her rail-thin arms and legs stuck out of a hand-me-down dress at least two sizes too big for her. Her clothes were tattered and her odor was strong and horrible. And to make matters all the worse, Rochelle had a disfiguring scar running across her face, leaving one of her eyes forever runny. She would be the target for every unkind comment and joke that children, the cruelty masters of the universe, could imagine.

From her appearance, I would have thought Rochelle was desperately poor. Imagine my surprise during the Open House when I met her father, a well-to-do business man in the community. He had tried the best way he knew how to raise his troubled daughter on his own, since her mother died when she was three. He, like the rest of her teachers, was floundering—desperately trying to help a person who was trying desperately to avoid that help.

My first encounter with Rochelle was unpleasant to say the least. On her first day of school—which was two weeks after everyone else had reported to school—Rochelle entered my room, promptly marched up to the first kid she spotted and in a loud voice announced he was in her seat. Since she had never been in my room before and since I had never assigned seats, what she said was false. No matter. It had its intended impact and immediately there was an unpleasant verbal exchange. With disbelieving eyes I watched as Rochelle—a scrawny bantam hen of a person—squared off with a linebacker of our football team.

"Come on!" she screamed in an unattractive squeaky voice. "Get outta my chair and fight me, you wimp!"

Harold just rolled his eyes and hunkered down more deeply in his chair. "You'd best be outta my face," he breathed slowly.

I gently touched Rochelle's shoulder to get her attention. She swung around with such force and malice, that I almost could see stars before a blow was even struck.

"Don't you touch me! Don't you ever touch me!" she erupted.

"Okay, okay," I said, backing off. "It's just I have a perfectly good seat over here with your name on it." I gestured in the direction of her chair, and she—not wanting to lose face I'd imagine—sashayed over, scowling and snarling back at Harold all the way.

Every day it was something like that. Before every lesson, I had to intercede in some kind of verbal assault initiated by Rochelle. One day, she accused her neighbor of stealing her notebook paper. The fact that it had been blown off her desk didn't even occur to her. She was ready to duke it out with poor unsuspecting Andrew, a tall, lanky kid. Another time she began yelling at someone who had tripped over her bookbag, left in the middle of the aisle where one could easily step on it.

"Excuse me," Flosette said as her large frame almost fell over the bookbag when her feet got tangled in the mess Rochelle had created by her desk.

"You old cow, bitch! You stepped on my foot!" Rochelle said between clenched teeth. She jumped from her desk and drew herself up to her full height in a threatening, hostile posture.

"Who you callin' a cow and a bitch?" Flosette countered, straightening up to her full and impressive height. I could feel the tension mounting as the scrawny Rochelle was about to take on a girl about twice her size.

"All right, ladies," I said, moving over to intercede if necessary. "We have a lot to cover today. You have an exam very soon, you know."

Without so much as a nod or any kind of conciliatory gesture, Rochelle turned her back to Flosette and sat with a thud in her seat. Flosette just shook her head in disbelief and then took her seat as well. How anyone could like Rochelle after all of her unkindnesses would be amazing, but I did come to like her, and it happened much to my surprise.

We were getting into the pre-Civil War literature when we got to the lesson on Sojourner Truth. Even the postage stamp-sized photograph reminded me of Rochelle—strong-willed, defiant and strangely ancient. It seemed only natural that I would have Rochelle read the passage to the class, and that was when it happened. Rochelle became a different person to me. Maybe even to herself. She took on the mantle of Sojourner so completely that I was all but transported to another time. So was the class. Her animated speech and empathetic gestures made her likeable to me for the first time, and I sensed it was the same for the other students as well.

"Ain't I a woman?" Rochelle said with great power and reality. And Sojourner's words became Rochelle's words, and it was hard to distinguish between the two. When she finished, there was a reverent silence. I was almost overcome. I had to fight the lump forming in my throat.

Finally I said, "Rochelle, . . . that was . . . excellent!"

Murmurs of agreement rippled through the room, and for the first time ever, I saw Rochelle smile. With a smile on her face, all the ugliness melted away and a totally new person stood before me. It was amazing.

"You have a real gift for acting," I continued. "Have you ever thought about joining a little theater?"

Some students' faces looked over at me with incredulity. Their mouths fell open. Their eyes got wide.

"No, ma'am."

"Well, you should consider it. As a matter of fact, I'd love to see you at the poetry reading on Wednesday. I have some poems I was going to read to the group, but you'd do them so much better than I could ever do. Would you at least think about coming?"

Heads swung in her direction to see what she might say. Then with a beaming smile, she simply said, "Yeah, I'll be there."

When Wednesday came and the poets were assembled for the informal readings we had each week during the lunch period, Rochelle walked through the library door a transformed person. She wore flattering blue jeans and red pullover sweater. Her hair had been plaited in attractive little cornrows, her face had the slightest hint of powder and she smelled of lavender soap.

"Rochelle," I said energetically, "I'm so glad you could make it." Before it got too mushy and I embarrassed her away, I went over and handed her a fistful of poems I had had typed for her. "Just look these over and pick a few to read to the group."

She took them and nodded. She never said a word. While she glanced over the material, I returned to the podium to handle a few organizational matters; then I opened the meeting.

"Poets, I have a real treat for you today. I'd like to introduce to you, Rochelle Freeman. She is going to read some Gwendolyn Brooks poems for you."

Rochelle slowly rose to come to the podium and paused dramatically after she had taken her place. Then, with the skill of a seasoned actor, she opened her mouth and filled the room with a silky, sultry voice. Within seconds the group was mesmerized by the sound and the transformation that took place as she took on whatever persona the poems called for.

Rochelle's voice was "real cool" as the gin-swigging, pool-playing characters in the first poem. It was a cowboy's in the second and it became an old woman's in "The Bean Eaters." It was an extraordinary time, and Rochelle was able to bask in the warm applause that came at the end of each selection.

Then, as if it couldn't get more amazing, the most moving moment of all occurred. Rochelle asked if she might read some of her own poems to the group.

"Absolutely," I answered before I could let anyone else respond.

She began with a rather amateurish teenage love poem that was all in the head and not anywhere in the heart, but it wasn't bad for a kid of her age and experience. Then she came to a wonderful piece about her grandmother's kitchen and how that woman's life's work seemed to be totally within the confines of that "warm and happy room." She called it "Neena's Bein' Place" and it was so well drawn that I could almost smell the aromas of apple pies baking and cornbread cooling on sideboards. The poem itself was not very long, but its sentiment was powerfully rendered.

All of us were extremely impressed. The applause was not exactly thunderous. We were in a library, after all; but there was no denying that Rochelle was quite a poet. She also was becoming more than that wildly angry child in my first period class. She smiled at all the praise that was heaped upon her and suddenly she became beautiful.

She read a few more poems. Then as we were nearing the end, she finished by reading very dramatically another student's poems. Passersby began to stop and listen. Even the principal, Mr. Ward, stopped and took a seat and stayed until the end, an uncharacteristic move since he was usually on his lunch duty rounds at that time of the day. His approval came through in the faint smile that crossed his usually solemn face.

Rochelle had read for the entire block of time allotted to the lunch period. At the end, there was considerable applause, and every person in attendance went up to congratulate and praise her for her fine performances. It was her moment, and I regretted having to hurry everyone up so I could close off the library room and get to my next class before the bell.

"Rochelle," I said, carefully putting my arm around her shoulders for a tentative hug, "you were wonderful! And your poems! What can I say? They are wonderful! Won't you please come again?"

She returned my hug hard and said, "Thanks. I'll be here."

LESSON 4

"Do I feel joy again?" cried Arthur, wondering at himself.
"Methought the germ of it was dead in me! O Hester, thou
are my better angel! I seem to have flung myself—sick, sin-
stained, and sorrow-blackened—down upon these forest-
leaves, and to have risen up all made anew, and with new
powers to glorify Him that hath been merciful! This is already
the better life! Why did we not find it sooner?"

The Scarlet Letter
Nathaniel Hawthorne

Every time I come to this part of *The Scarlet Letter*, I
almost believe Hester and her poor Arthur will actually
leave the great forest and escape the ravages of sin, sorrow, and
Roger Chillingworth. Every time I read Arthur's words about
his feeling joy again, I am filled with hope. Even though I've
read the book countless times, I still desperately hope these
lovers will be together and find peace in the communion of
their shared secret. And every time I read the book, I am again
disappointed that the ending doesn't change. I almost always

cry when Arthur dies in Hester's arms, and I put the book down with a real sense of loss.

It still astonishes me that something written over a hundred years ago about something that supposedly happened three hundred years ago can still move me so. I guess the power of the written word is truly mightier than swords and death and time, and I guess that is why I became an English teacher. I have always wanted to open the eyes of children to the ideas of the past so their life-journeys can be easier to travel and hopefully more satisfying.

But I was troubled that six or seven student heads were down on their desks as we discussed the chapter they were to have read the night before.

"Come on, Robert," I said to the nearest fallen head. "Look at page 185. What do you see happening there in the forest?"

Lifting his sleep-wrinkled face from his folded arms, he said, "Man, I don't need this dumb book. What's it ever going to do for me, anyway?"

Robert was long and lanky and full of mischief. Usually he couldn't be quiet and needed to be the center of attention, but his sleeping in class could only mean he worked late at his job last night. Since he did not have the money that most of the other students did, as evidenced by his not-so-stylish clothes, he had to work as a stock clerk at the local Dixie Dale Grocery Store. He could easily get to college with his grades, but he would be there only with the help of scholarships and only if he would wake up.

I probably should have just let him sleep, because he could be terribly disruptive. Once when I was trying hard to explain the intricacies of comma usage, Robert interrupted me three times to tell me that Jesus was a black man, apparently to see what I'd say. Finally, I told him I didn't care what color Jesus was; his race was unimportant to me. It took the wind right out of his sails when I refused to argue, and he was crestfallen for the rest of the class period.

Today, he had wanted to sleep, and whether it said

somewhere in my contract I must awaken all students who fall asleep or I was just feeling a perverse sense of orneriness, I insisted he stay awake.

"Robert, dear," I said as calmly as I could. "In this English class we have to study American literature. In it, one is supposed to read classic books of literature. Eventually, you all will be taking the Advanced Placement Test next year, and if you all haven't read books like this, then you'll be considerably disadvantaged. You then may not make an acceptable score and you won't be able to get into college or earn a scholarship to save your parents money, and everyone will be mad, not at you, but at me. But that's beside the point. Why must I always defend the curriculum to you? You say you want to go to college and you must realize that you have certain things you must do before they will let you go there. Why is this always a problem with you? Surely you knew this would be the situation when you signed up for this honors class."

"But no one told me these books would be so boring when I signed up."

Soft laughter spread through the room.

"How can you tell if it is boring if you haven't read any of it?" I asked.

"Oooooo!" the class breathed out in unison.

"She got you good, Bro," Joshua, a handsome, stylishly dressed young man, said with a laugh.

"I read some of it," Robert protested, "it's just that it's so white."

I could feel that new kind of anger rising in me. Once again it all boiled down to an issue of race. Words could come down from heaven on stone tablets, and if they didn't have "written by an African-American" stamped on it somewhere, Robert would use that as an excuse to find it boring and get out of his reading assignments.

My tone was cold when I said, "I didn't necessarily choose these books, but they are the ones most frequently mentioned on the AP exams, and for some strange reason, I thought you'd appreciate being competitive with all the thousands of white students with whom you'll be competing. Don't you want to know what they know?"

Before I said anything more in my defense, Leanne's hand went up. Of all the students I have ever taught so far, Leanne was closest to my heart. We were considerably different in age and appearance. She was younger than her counterparts, having skipped over an elementary grade in an accelerated program. Very slight, with a smooth dark complexion and soft, curly close-cropped hair, she was neatly and carefully dressed in a floral dress that was not at all ostentatious. Her quiet way of viewing the world was quite similar to the way I saw it, and I felt as if I had somehow found a soulmate.

"Yes, Leanne?"

"I don't think this book is boring," she said. "I cried at the end when Arthur dies in Hester's arms."

My heart gave a silent shout of joy.

" . . . and I don't mind that these people are white. I think there is something all people can learn from this story."

"You're always frontin', aren't you, Leanne," Robert growled playfully at her.

Leanne was not ruffled. She just smiled. The class's attention was now riveted upon her to see what response she would make to his insult.

"Maybe I front and maybe I don't, but that doesn't change the fact that there is something to be learned from this book."

"Like what? That white people have always and always will look down on single mothers? Like welfare mothers don't set their tongues to wagging about how immoral they are? How immoral all blacks are?"

"No, like single mothers are the moral superiors of the men who made them mothers."

"Now, just where does it say that?" Joshua asked.

"It doesn't say it directly, but just look how the story turns out. Hester isn't eaten up by guilt as Arthur is. Hester is strong and lives to be an old woman. Arthur dies broken and defeated. This makes me think that women, who can't hide their sins the way men can, are forced to deal with them in the open. It is what makes us strong."

"Strong?" Robert said. "What makes you think women, the reason why we men fell from God's grace in the first place, are so strong?"

Numerous groans went up from the class. Robert's frequent "sermons" were not always well received or appreciated.

"From experience," Leanne said.

"Experience?" Robert started to laugh.

"Yes, experience. See, Hester is a lot like my own mama. She's a lot like the mamas of many of us in here. My mama was all set to go to college and carve out an exciting life for herself when she got pregnant. With me."

She dramatically played to the crowd of faces that now looked in her direction. Many of the students were nodding in agreement with each thing she said.

"I was kinda like my mother's 'pearl of great price,' if you know what I mean. Instead of aborting me or dumping me in a ditch or leaving me with an old auntie, she stood by me even though she lost everything she ever wanted for herself. She never heard from my father, and her own mama threw her out of the house. We had to live with my great-grandmother for the first three years of my life.

"And don't think the whites have a monopoly on cruelness to single mothers. Our being black didn't stop the ugly talk that went on behind our backs, either."

"That's only 'cause your mama dresses you so funny," Robert said almost playfully, as if he were trying to lighten the heaviness of the moment he had caused.

Laughter followed, and Leanne laughed too.

"Coming from a man wearing a holey tee shirt and some kind of K-Mart Special pants, I'm really insulted."

"Ooooo!" the student chorus said.

"Okay, okay," I say, trying to get the class back on task. "That's enough of that for today. Back to Arthur and Hester in the forest."

The lesson continued until the bell rang, and Robert did manage to keep his head up and his eyes open for the rest of the class. I managed to appreciate the wonder of a perceptive and open mind.

LESSON 5

Once upon a midnight dreary, while I pondered, weak and
     weary,
Over many a quaint and curious volume of forgotten lore—
While I nodded, nearly napping, suddenly there came a
     tapping,
As of someone gently rapping . . . .

"The Raven"
Edgar Allan Poe

Standard eleventh graders are often a real challenge to teach,
even for the best of teachers, much less for those who are
fresh out of college. Part of the reason for the difficulty of this
particular standard eleventh-grade class was that it occurred towards
the end of the day when we were all tired. Another reason this
class was so hard to teach was most of the children in it were from
the skills center. That meant they were not pursuing further
academic training after high school. For the most part these kids
were going directly into trades—plumbing, auto mechanics,
cosmetology, child care. They spent the bulk of their day doing

hands-on type work and then came here for their "book learnin'" in the afternoon. Of course, the only type of book these kids ever wanted to read was comic books, and the only type of writing they wanted to do was the type connected with the procurement of a job.

When it came time for me to teach "The Raven," one of my all-time favorite poems, a flurry of groans filled the room, and I knew I was in for a difficult ride. To make matters worse, it was Homecoming Week and on this particular day, everyone was to be dressed in costume.

Homecoming Week in any high school is a real treat for teachers. To begin with, it is incredibly distracting. Along with hall decorating and king and queen elections, there were themes to be played out on each of the days of that week.

Monday had been Boy/Girl Switch Day when the girls dressed like boys and the boys like girls. This proved to be the most distracting day. I could hardly teach anything when I'd look out into the class and see the young men swinging their hips provocatively all the way down the aisles and crossing their stockinged legs ever so effeminately. It was all I could do to keep from collapsing into a fit of giggles when the young women so accurately captured the swagger and gestures of the guys as they spoke in class.

Tuesday was Jamaican Holiday Day and everyone came dressed in tourist shirts and straw hats. Wednesday was Teacher Impersonation Day, or as some of us teachers call it "The Day of 1,000 Insults." I was a little hurt no one impersonated me until, of course, I saw how they mocked Mr. Jennings. Numerous students wore long black pants with chalk dust rubbed around the pockets, and they wore horn-rimmed glasses at the ends of their noses and stooped over as they walked. They had poor old Mr. Jennings pegged, but he was such a good sport about it all. He was laughing and talking about it in the lounge. I guess his students really loved him to go to such lengths to get his gestures right.

In keeping with the spirit of Homecoming Week, I was doing my part for Thursday's Sixties Day. I was decked out in clothes I had bought at a local thrift store—a pair of bell-bottom pants, a dashiki shirt, and sandals. I had drawn a peace symbol on my face with eye liner, and my hair hung long and straight under my bandanna headband. One can easily imagine how difficult it is to command respect from anybody, much less high school students, when so dressed; but there I was in all my hippie glory, trying to make Edgar Allan Poe relevant.

"Edgar Allan Poe is one of the all-time greats," I said, starting the lesson.

Luscious, a good-natured class clown, let out a loud and long yawn.

Undeterred, I continued. "Poe has an interesting story. Do any of you know anything about good old Edgar?"

"Ms. Webster, what are you dressed up as?" Luscious asked, as I watched his eyes travel the length of my body from head to toe and back.

"I'm a flower child—you know, The '60s and all," I said. "Now, what do you know about Poe?"

"You look more like a love child to me," he said thoughtfully. One small giggle erupted somewhere and then the room fell silent.

"Come on, class. Doesn't anybody know anything about Edgar Allan Poe?"

There was another long pause, until Vermellia, one of the brighter students, said, "He was a drug addict, wasn't he?"

"That's a good point, Vermellia," I said. "Poe was probably an alcoholic, but there is not much that really substantiates his addiction to opium. Poe has gotten a lot of bad press, thanks to a scandal sheet published about him after he died by one of his enemies. It is true he is known for his macabre stories and themes. After all, his young wife died shortly after they were married and it had a terrible impact upon him, but who wouldn't be saddened by that?"

There was more silence. Three heads had nodded all the way

down to the desk tops. Another two had fallen backward against the wall. Soon I expected snoring to fill the void, and I just wasn't in the mood to let that happen.

"Reginald?" I said to one of the closest sunken heads.

"What?" he answered sleepily as his head jerked up.

"Please go over to the wooden cabinet over there and beat on it."

"Say what?"

"You heard me. Go beat on my cabinets."

As Reginald slowly, almost cautiously, rose to move to the back of the class where the cabinets were, the other heads rose from their sleepy state. All eyes became riveted upon the large teenager ambling to the back of the classroom.

"What is she doing?" I heard Luscious whisper.

"She's nuts," his neighbor whispered back.

"Now, Reginald," I said. "Do you know what RAP music is?"

The classroom exploded with incredulous laughter.

"Yes, I know what RAP music is, Mrs. Webster."

"And you can do a rap beat on my cabinets?"

"I guess so."

"Then do it."

Gingerly at first, and then with gathering strength, Reginald began booming out a rap rhythm that soon had heads bobbing with the beat. Once he had established the rhythm, I began reading "The Raven," matching each poetic accent with the rhythm drummed on the cabinet.

I moved out in front of the class, book in hand and listened for the laughter I was sure would come. It didn't. Instead, I heard a female voice in the right corner pick up the poem with me. Then another voice, and then another until the entire class was rappin' "The Raven" as if we were making a video for BETV.

Boom tah tah boom tah tah boom tah tah boom boom.

Over and over it went until the chorus was quite loud, and some of the kids were rising out of their seats, dancing to the beat, arms up in the air. Strange faces could be seen peering into the window of my door. Obviously our good time was spilling out over the transom, under the door and through the walls.

It was wild and wonderful, and it was all I could do to keep from dropping a syllable or tripping over my tongue; but I was committed now. Or maybe I should be.

Boom tah tah boom tah tah boom tah tah boom boom.

Slowly we inched along until we were halfway, three quarters of the way, and then all the way through the 108 lines of the poem. As the last line reverberated off the walls, the room erupted into cheers, and I took a well-earned bow.

"Let's do it again!" the cry went up. "Let's do it again!"

Since this was the first time I had seen any life from this class, I could hardly refuse.

"All right," I agreed, "but this time, let's change the rhythm. Let's see if a different cadence can work as well as that one. Luscious? You want to try it this time?"

"Sure!" Luscious said, jumping to his feet, and soon we were off on another rhythmical journey.

Boom pa ta da Boom pa ta da Boom pa ta da Boom pa ta da.

This time, my door actually opened, and students from the hall and then other classes began to wander in and take up the poem, clapping their hands and stomping their feet. I felt a thrill of panic at the thought an administrator might not approve and find this too disruptive an activity. Then, I let the dread pass from me. This seemed to be making poetry a real and viable entity to these eleventh-grade students. I couldn't stop what was proving to be a powerful lesson.

Again we inched along the lines of the poem and when we came to the tumultuous end, the cheer that went up was deafening.

"All right, class!" I had to yell. "All right! Back to your seats! And you all over there! Back to your own classrooms!" I yelled at the intruders. Slowly, the crowd began to break up.

"Hey, man, that was really good," Reginald said to me, over the noise. "You really know how to teach good."

I blushed at the compliment. "Thanks," I said as the bell rang and the students, still swimming with the rhythms of the lesson, walked to the cadence of a poet long dead. I felt wonderful! I felt like I had taught that one "pretty good" too.

OCTOBER

LESSON 6

The mass of men lead lives of quiet desperation.

Walden

Henry David Thoreau

I f it had not been for a very powerful poem that was left upon my desk one day, I would never have come to know Yasmina as a considerable talent and not just another pretty face. I also would never have come to know just what it is some of my students must go through to make it through a day.

Yasmina reminded me of an Ethiopian princess, her carriage being so regal and sedate. Her creamy, caramel-colored skin was always beautifully complemented by the intricate designs in her hair style. Sometimes, she wore long plaits with golden bobbles at the end. Sometimes the cornrows were collected in a bun situated at the crown of her head. Sometimes her hair was loose and soft to her shoulders. In any event, Yasmina was always beautiful, and this fact amazed me, especially after I discovered her poetry.

The poem that had been left on my desk told of how her stepfather, who was drunk and on a rampage of jealousy, had killed her mother. Yasmina's poem told all about it in a matter-of-fact tone, and I am sure my eyes must have grown wider and wider as the horror of her recollection revealed itself upon the page. At first, I was morbidly fascinated, I have to admit, but as I read line after line of despairing detail, I began to feel the gravity of her words.

She spoke of how she and her three little brothers huddled together in the corner of the shabby, dingy living room as the "monster-sized man" beat her mother with "giant fists" and then stabbed her over and over again with a "filthy, rusted pocket-knife." His "hunter-animal" eyes stared at the children who "screamed like angels on fire." Then, he closed his "evil" eyes and slept while Yasmina crawled on hands and knees to find the phone to call for help.

This scene still haunts her, the poem said, and she can never close her eyes that it doesn't fill her mind with the fear and rage that will not leave her. In one stanza she even said she sometimes wishes that "the monster" had killed her instead, especially when the "nightmare men come each night/and prowl around her room."

I was breathless when I came to the end of her poem. How is it possible any human being would have to have such visions, such memories, such wishes? How is it possible any child has had to endure such an unthinkable event?

I wasn't sure how I was going to approach Yasmina after reading this poem. I sensed she wanted desperately to talk to me about her poetry and her life, but I didn't want to scare her away. Adults sometimes get carried away when a child makes an overture. I didn't want to betray her confidence by showing this work to a guidance counselor, either. Still, I was uneasy about her talk of death and her desire to die when the "nightmare men" came. I had to find a way to let her reach out for whatever help I could give, and I figured this poem was her first step.

I thought I might write a response back to her on the poem. I wrote my answer first on a separate piece of paper so I'd say just the right thing in just the right way. It took me almost an hour to think, compose, and then rewrite the final response onto the back of her poem. I said:

Your poetry is absolutely spellbinding, Yasmina. I was very moved by your words and your topic. With your command of the language and your sensitivity to the details of events, you shall be a great writer when you grow up.

I can only imagine how horrible it was for you to live through such an event. And your little brothers? How have they managed?

Isn't it wonderful we have writing so we can get our sorrows out on paper where they are not so scary; where we can put them into perspective? Maybe you could write some more poems about your thoughts and feelings? I would love to see them. Maybe you wouldn't mind if I shared your work with other students or our class? Maybe you would become a part of the poetry group and share your insights with us all?

Please know I am here if ever you want to talk, and you have my home phone number. I am here if you ever want me to see another of your poems. Please write more!!

The next day as I was returning old homework papers to students, I returned Yasmina's poem with my comments carefully written on it. I tried surreptitiously to see her face and monitor it for a reaction as I moved about the room issuing papers. I could tell when she was reading my comments and then a small, gentle smile crossed her face. I knew I had done the right thing.

Before long, I was bombarded with page after page of Yasmina poetry—some of it great, some of it very amateurish, but all of it touching and genuine. We began a kind of correspondent relationship—she'd write a poem and I'd write my response. It worked well for a number of weeks, and finally she made her way to the poetry workshop where she would ask me to read her poems for her to the group. Tears quite often fell down the cheeks of the other poets, even our feisty Rochelle. A reverent silence instead of applause often filled the spaces between her poems. Soon, everyone had a favorite, and Yasmina "arrived" when the poetry group insisted she read her own work from now on.

Whether her "nightmare men" disappeared from her nights, I can only guess, but her school days were filled with a new verification for her feelings. She had poetry, and that was enough for her for the while.

LESSON 7

I know why the caged bird sings, ah me,
When his wing is bruised and his bosom sore—
When he beats his bars and he would be free;
It is not a carol of joy or glee,
But a prayer that he sends from his heart's deep core,
But a plea, that upward to Heaven he flings—
I know why the caged bird sings!

"Sympathy"
Paul Lawrence Dunbar

Juanita was one of the cutest students I had ever taught. She was all of four and a half feet tall and resembled an elementary student more than the high school junior she was. Her smile was winning and her charm was considerable. Her close cropped ebony hair complemented her soft, tawny features. Her clothes were not always the most stylish, but she was always neat, pressed and well-groomed. If it weren't for the fact that Juanita was a behavior problem, I guess she would go down as one of my favorite students.

Her major fault was she could not shut her mouth. Many a lesson or reading was interrupted by her incessant chatter. After a while that chatter could drive a grown woman to tears. Hers was a high pitched, loud screech at times, and it often felt like the sound of grinding metal machinery.

"Juanita!" I'd call out. "It is time to get to work. Chit-chat time is over."

"But, Mrs. Webster, I have to ask Angela just one more question, please. Please. Please!"

"Juanita, you have been asking Angela questions all morning long. It is time to do your work. Come on, now. Let's get to it."

"BUT, Mrs. Webster," she'd whine, "I really have to know what happened last . . ."

"Juanita," I'd whine back. "You really need to get to work."

She'd finally open her book and the second I'd turn my head, she'd be thick as thieves with her neighbor creating that machinery noise in tremendous volume. If this behavior had occurred only in a few isolated incidents, I would have been able to overlook it, but this was a daily ritual we went through until I finally had all the foolishness I could stand. I sent her to the guidance department for a little guidance.

Juanita was furious. How dare I single her out for treatment! Didn't other people in the class talk just as much as she did? And why didn't I just talk to her privately, huh? How come I had to send her to the depths of the office to talk to that fruity old counselor up there who was always into her business anyway?

When she came back from her counseling session, she pouted for about fifteen minutes and then forgot she was mad and started chattering again, as I stood before the class to give the next assignment.

"Do I have to send you to the dean this time to get you to be quiet?" I asked after stopping my lesson, pausing long enough to let her stop.

"What?"

"I need you to be quiet. I'm trying to teach."

"I wasn't talking."

"Well, then just what was it you were doing with your mouth?"

"Nothing."

"Well, then stop doing 'nothing' with your mouth or I'll be forced to put you out."

"Why you always picking on me?"

"I don't always pick on you. Now, be quiet or I'll have to send you to the dean."

"You just don't like me."

"That's it!"

I had tolerated all the back talk I could stand. I had reached my limit. Maybe I was feeling a little bit under the weather. Maybe not, but the incessant Juanita had pushed me over the brink. I wrote out the referral to the dean of discipline.

Juanita was horrified.

"I didn't do nothing to deserve that! I am a good student! I can't believe a bitch like you is ever allowed to teach!" she screamed.

Suddenly Rochelle came to my aid. "Watch how you talk to her!" she said, jumping to her feet as if to let Juanita have it but good.

"That's okay, Rochelle. I can handle this."

I just kept writing and put Juanita's slur into the report. I then got up, walked over to her seat, handed the referral to the child, and asked her to leave. She promptly tore the referral in half and threw it on the ground. The class was absolutely quiet, and I could see Rochelle pursing her lips and flaring her nostrils.

As I walked back to my desk, I paused at Rochelle's desk and gave her a reassuring smile. "It will be all right," I said to her quietly.

I then went out of the room, called for a hall monitor and asked that he personally escort a young lady to the dean. Mr. Harrington's hulking frame moved into the threshold of my class and that alone would have intimidated most people. Not Juanita. She wouldn't budge from her desk even after he came over and towered over her.

"Looks like I'm going to have to make an emergency call, little lady, if you don't cooperate."

Juanita glared at me, then him. She folded her arms over her chest. She wasn't going anywhere.

The monitor radioed over his walkie-talkie for the dean to come to Room 409 for a defiant student and then we waited. All the while Juanita mumbled under her breath about the "bitch" at the front of the class, that "honkie" who hates black children, that "disgusting, ugly white hag that doesn't understand nothin' about black children."

Rochelle trembled with controlled rage.

The monitor was close enough to hear every word. He said softly to Juanita, "I don't know about all that, little lady, but white or no, teachers don't ever deserve to be talked to like that and if you was my child, you'd be slapped up against that back wall right now."

His words, at least, got her to stop the mumbling. The word to describe Juanita's face when Sarah Weller, the Dean of Girls, walked in was "terrorized." Ms. Weller was a tall, thin, gray-haired matriarch in a purple floral dress who probably wielded the most power in this school building; even more than Mr. Ward, the principal. No one ever crossed or wanted to be crossed by Ms. Weller, and the expression that moved over the child's face proved this fact to be true in Juanita's mind at least. Suddenly I felt sorry for her.

"Come on, little girl," Ms. Weller said coldly when she got to my room and evaluated the situation. Juanita got up, bent and broken like a puppy with her tail between her legs. We didn't see her for five days. Five gloriously silent days. When the sixth day came, I decided I would move heaven and earth before I'd confront Juanita today. To help her stay quiet, I moved her closer to my desk and away from her usual talking temptations. Maybe this time, we'd be able to coexist.

Juanita did indeed stay quiet. She just put her head down on the desk and slept through the entire class. I guess she showed me.

The next day when she came to class, she once again put her

head down on the desk to sleep. I decided then that her grade was now in peril. After all, she had already been suspended for five days, she slept the sixth, and she hadn't been doing well initially. I knew I'd better act or I'd be guilty of picking on her where it really counts. I'd be letting her fail.

"Juanita," I whispered to her as I came near her desk to awaken her. "Juanita, I know this is a difficult class situation for you, but if you don't wake up, stay quiet and do your work, I'll be forced to call your mother to get her . . . ."

"NO! You can't do that!" she said loudly enough for the class to turn their heads in her direction. "I'll work, Mrs. Webster. See. I'm getting out my books and everything. I'll do whatever you say, just please don't call my mama."

I was surprised by the desperate nature of her reaction, especially after she had been so defiant in the past.

"Well," I remarked, "why don't you want me to talk to your mother?"

"Because she said if I get into any more trouble she won't let me sing in the talent contest at the church on Sunday."

"You're a singer, Juanita?"

"Yes, ma'am. Gospel mostly."

"I didn't know. You'll have to sing for us sometime."

Without making another sound, she bent down over her work, and I moved on to help other students with their assignments. For the entire class period, there wasn't a sound from her side of the room. As a matter of fact, I didn't hear a peep out of Juanita for at least a week.

I was at my between-class post in the hall one day when I felt a tap on my shoulder from someone behind me.

"Juanita," I said as I turned and saw her standing there smiling.

"I won!" she beamed.

"You won the talent contest?"

"Yes! First Place!" she said, overflowing with joy.

"Well, why don't you sing your winning number for the class today? I'd really love to hear your singing voice."

"I don't know," she said, suddenly shy.

"Ah, come on. If you could sing for all those judges at the contest and all the people in your church, you can sing for your class."

"I'll think about it," she said. Then she turned and bounced happily down the hall. I didn't see her again until it was time for class.

"Today, class, I have a real treat for you. Before we get started on our papers, Juanita is going to perform her First Place solo act for us right here this morning. Juanita."

She shook her head as the class clapped, cheered and egged her on. No. No, she kept telling us.

Finally I said, "Come on, Juanita."

"I just can't."

"Why not?"

"Because I'll laugh if I have to look at the people's faces."

"Just close your eyes, then," someone offered.

"Or you could turn around and face the blackboard," offered another.

After a few more seconds of coaxing, Juanita was at the front of the classroom and turned toward the wall so all we could see was her back. She opened her mouth and let out the most glorious sound. Not a machinery grinding noise, but a lovely, fluid deepness which vibrated in the hollow of my soul. It echoed soulfully off the wall and seemed to move around the room on angel wings.

"Sometimes I feel like a motherless child," she sang verse after verse for the silent and extremely appreciative audience. I was enthralled and overwhelmed. A tear ran down my cheek, and I tried ever so carefully to remove it before anyone could see.

"Look! Mrs. Webster is crying," I heard Rochelle whisper to her neighbor.

I just kept on listening, however; and when her song was over, Juanita turned at last to face us. She took a little bow.

The class offered wild applause and cheers. I clapped loudly as well.

"Wasn't that wonderful, class? Well done, Juanita! No wonder you won the contest! That was absolutely lovely!"

As we passed each other to go back to our everyday places, I said, "Juanita, you're going to grow up to be a famous singer, I bet."

"Thank you, Mrs. Webster," she said. And from that day forward, she never spoke out of turn again, and her grinding machinery voice went away from my ears forever.

LESSON 8

I hear America Singing, the varied carols I hear,
Those of mechanics, each one singing his as it should be
blithe and strong,
The carpenter singing his as he measures his plank or beam,
The mason singing his as he makes ready for work, or leaves
off work,
The boatman singing what belongs to him in his boat, the
deck hand singing on the steamboat deck,
The shoemaker singing as he sits on his bench, the hatter
singing as he stands,
The woodcutter's song, the ploughboy's on his way in the
morning, or at noon intermission or at sundown,
The delicious singing of the mother, or of the young wife at
work, or of the girl sewing or washing,
Each singing what belongs to him or her and to none else,
The day what belongs to the day—at night the party of
young fellows, robust, friendly,
Singing with open mouths their strong melodious songs.

"I Hear America Singing"
Walt Whitman

The first pep rally I had attended as a non-student happened while I was interning at Wakulla County High during the basketball season. The Rebels were about to win the state championship, and the principal had decided the students needed to send the team off with a rousing display of support. I didn't think much about the experience. The kids shuffled in slowly, but it was, after all, the end of the day. A few perky cheerleaders bounced around trying to enliven the crowd, but it seemed a futile effort at best. The small band played a thin, wispy rendition of Notre Dame's fight song over and over, and when the team members were introduced, each received varied amounts of minimal applause. Then we were encouraged to participate in a cheer or two, which most students read lethargically from photocopies hastily provided by the cheerleaders. It was an unextraordinary event, to say the least.

My first pep rally at Dunbar was an altogether different experience. As I entered the gymnasium, the floors and walls literally vibrated with powerful rhythms from a large, loud band with an exceptional drum corps. As the stands filled with students, a rhythm began as the kids took their seats. One side started the chant. "Seen-yahs!" Stomp. Stomp. "Seen-yahs!" Stomp. Stomp.

The opposing side was not to be outdone, so they took up another chant. "June-yahs!" Stomp. Stomp. "June-yahs!" Stomp. Stomp.

The noise was deafening when all the drummers took up the rhythm, and then a lone tuba belted out an impromptu melody that matched the chants. Everyone and everything was swaying.

The sophomores didn't have much of a chance to be heard in this celebration, and the poor freshmen wandered in, eyes wide and mouths open. So did I, I suppose.

Of course, this was for the football team, the mighty Dunbar Vikings, and maybe football teams inspire more enthusiasm at pep rallies than basketball teams do. I wouldn't know for sure until the spring, but this display of devotion was remarkable. What a spectacle! And this was at the end of the day!

I started to take note of the different types of children I saw there. Other than the different classes, there seemed to be other divisions. There were the Army ROTC kids in uniform, who stood sentry watches at all the entrances and lined the wall for crowd control. There were the cheerleaders, who seemed most serious about what they were doing. There was a no-nonsense attitude in the way they executed their cheers. Not many of them smiled.

The band consisted of many instruments and players who swayed even when they were not actively playing their instruments. They wore matching tee shirts and shorts, and some band members had flags that they swirled and twirled in unison. The flag corps was a flashy, almost flamboyant, group. I think I even saw one male in their ranks, but I soon lost sight of that person in the distractions that competed for my attention.

The football players, dressed in their jerseys without pads, still formed a considerable wall in one section of the bleachers. I could just make out the massive forms of Percy and Avery, who stood together in the stands. Harold from my first period was a giant presence two rows behind them.

On the opposite and farthest wall was a group of "cut-ups" wearing white tee shirts and smirky faces, causing teachers to begin a slow migration in their direction to help keep them in line. I could see Robert among them, and I thought I could make out Luscious.

Suddenly, an undisclosed voice came on over an antiquated sound system and in a feedback-filled announcement said, "Please stand for the presentation of the colors."

Silence fell over the once noisy group as the ROTC color guard came marching in with the flags. They slowly proceeded down the wooden floor as the cheerleaders covered their hearts with their pompons, the football players covered their numbers with massive hands. More militant youths raised clenched fists in the air as their salute. The rest of the crowd stood silently.

After the colors were presented, the band started "The Star Spangled Banner," and one clear, melodious voice on the public address system led us in the singing. It was enormously moving. I tingled all over and could feel emotion slowly coming to my eyes. Carefully and—I hoped—without anyone noticing, I removed a tissue from my purse just in case any tears should fall and betray my swelling feelings.

Just when I thought I had seen it all, the place went wild with activity. In a roar that did not quit until they left the floor, male dancers in army boots took the center of the floor and began a wild, stomping, but synchronized, dance. Girls squealed and acted like they were fainting. Boys bellowed their approval. I later learned that this was "steppin'" and a high art form in some communities.

I'd never seen anything like it in my life, although there was something tremendously primitive about it. The dancers were downright sexual in most of their movements. It truly was exciting, but I was a bit uncomfortable. I just couldn't believe that in Bible Belt, Jacksonville, Florida, such gyrations would long be tolerated in a school assembly. I had this fear that a school board member would walk in and then have the place raided or something awful like that. I was amazed at how normal the other teachers seemed to feel these dances were.

I must be getting old, I thought. When I stopped and thought about it, I remembered how "dirty" my parents thought my generation's dances were. Maybe I just needed to get used to this.

Soon the dancers were replaced by the flag girls and one boy who marched out their dance in typical synchronized marching routines. Cheerleaders followed with their pyramid extravaganza, and then one last steppin' group performed. They were not so good as the first and literally got "booed." Rough crowd, I thought.

Finally, the rousing fight song filled the air and all voices took it up. The vivacity was overwhelming. My skin crawled and I again tingled all over. I even began to quiver at the base of my stomach. It was a glory to behold!

When the final bell rang, the crowd poured out of their seats and the pep rally was over. I was exhausted, but tremendously uplifted. How could we not win the game?

LESSON 9

"Spek, swete bird, I noot not wher thou art."
This Nicholas anon let flee a fart,
As greet as it had been a thonder-dent.

"The Miller's Tale"
The Canterbury Tales
Geoffrey Chaucer

"Now that we have finished the prologue to *The Canter-bury Tales*," I said to my seniors one fine October day, "we will begin reading some of the actual tales of the pilgrims; but before we start with the required 'Knight's Tale,' there is just one thing I must ask you to do. Actually, I am asking you not to do something. I don't care which tales you read on your own, so long as you don't—and I mean it, now—don't read either of 'The Miller's Tales.'"

"Since when does a teacher tell students not to read something?" Mario whispered to his neighbor. "I think you're up to something, Ms. Webster," he said more loudly for us all to hear.

I smiled. I was indeed up to something. I was using some

reverse psychology in an effort to excite my students about their next arduous reading task—*The Canterbury Tales*. Of course, we would not be reading the Middle English version, thank goodness. We had a nice Nevill Coghill translation into contemporary English, but sometimes modern teenagers ignore the older stories. I guess they feel anything that isn't on TV or been made into a movie isn't worth their time or attention. My plan was to "briar-patch" them into reading something they probably would really enjoy by using Br'er Rabbit's legendary trick.

"It's just that I can't—in all good conscience—require you to read something as gross, disgusting, and nasty as the Miller's tales. It has been suggested the Miller's tales be deleted from all the textbooks because so many parents don't want their children reading about such things. However," I paused here for effect, "I have to admit the Miller's stories are some of the funniest stories I've ever read. They are so dirty."

Here I laughed and gave them a wink. "I think some of the dirtiest jokes in the world have found their basis in the stories of the Canterbury pilgrims. But still, I have to ask you not to read pages 156 to 170, because your parents would have a fit if they thought I had required you to read this."

My strategy had begun to work. Immediately, I could hear the pages being flipped frantically as students throughout the room began gleaning the pages for the juicy, ribald tidbits I supposedly was trying to hide from them. I was elated. My plan was working just beautifully, when all of a sudden, Avery made his presence known.

Avery was one of those quiet, amicable souls who drift in and out of classes. A teacher would hardly even know that he was ever in the classroom except that papers bearing his name appeared in the stacks of assignments. If it weren't for the fact that Avery was huge, I might not have noticed him at all. He was well over six feet and close to 300 pounds. He reminded me of a big, cuddly teddy bear the way he lumbered into the room, but he hardly made a sound all year. Except for that October day when he passed gas loudly and long, leaving no doubt as to what the sound was and who was responsible.

This sort of thing is usually more likely to happen in an elementary school, I had been told. The younger students do not always have proper control over their bodies just yet. In a grammar school, I might have expected such an event; and if I had expected such an event, I might have been vaguely aware of what to do and been prepared to deal with it appropriately.

In preparing for certification to teach senior high, I was never instructed on how to deal with "farting" episodes. Had such an episode happened to someone when I was in school, I was sure he or she would have been driven out of town on a rail. Had it happened to me, I would have begged for death. I never even dreamed such a thing could or would happen in my classroom. But it did.

More amazing than the actual event itself was the reaction of the students. I was shocked when the whole room erupted into a chaotic melee. Masses of students jumped from their desks and literally ran to the opposite side of the room. Desks were knocked over and misaligned. Papers and books fell to the floor. Boys let out cries of "Oh, man!!!" and the girls did no better. Everyone held his or her nose or covered his or her face.

"Jesus, Avery!! You been eatin' government cheese again!!" Mario yelled. There was muffled laughter since no one wanted to take a deep breath.

I tried to regain order by admonishing those who had swarmed across the rows to get away from Avery's immediate area, but by this time, his aroma had wafted up into my part of the room. It was all I could do to keep from gagging, myself.

"Go . . . back to your . . . seats!" I said. " . . . Settle dow . . . down!"

Avery, who was left all alone on his side of the room, hadn't batted an eye. He didn't even look up from his book. He sat there reading from his copy of *The Canterbury Tales* and doing the assignment I had written on the board earlier.

I went over to the door and opened it to let in whatever fresh air there can be found in a windowless, air-conditioned high school. I stood briefly inhaling the fetid hall air as if it were from a blossoming spring meadow. Then, I realized I was being selfish.

"Class," I said, as I turned back into the room. "Why don't we make our own pilgrimage to the outside, and once we get to the courtyard, each person must tell a tale just as if we were pilgrims ourselves."

Unlike my many other bright-idea assignments, this one met with no resistance. Hurriedly, students collected their belongings and rushed out of my room, down the hall and out the exit to the senior courtyard.

Quite by accident, I discovered a great way to teach and make relevant the ancient journey written about so long ago. The whole class and I spent a pleasant class period in the lovely fall morning as we told jokes and family stories. We laughed a lot and, of course, Avery—whom no one would sit near—attained the dubious title of "Nicholas" from the few who defied me and read the Miller's tales anyway.

NOVEMBER

LESSON 10

If you can walk with crowds and keep your virtue,
Or walk with kings—nor lose the common touch,
If neither foes nor loving friends can hurt you,
If all men count with you, but none too much;
If you can fill the unforgiving minute
With sixty seconds' worth of distance run,
Yours is the earth and everything that's in it,
And—which is more—you'll be a man, my son!

"If____"
Rudyard Kipling

It was hard to tell from where I sat just who was in the flag corps. Also, my eyes watered from the blustery, cold wind that whipped around me as I sat watching the half-time performance in the Dunbar football stadium. From where I sat shivering, the flag corps resembled little red-clad stick figures swirling and swishing their flags in interesting patterns set by the rhythms of the band. But as the performers came off the field in my direction, there was no mistaking who it was I saw there. Joshua, the dapper young man from my honors 11 class, proudly swirled his flag along with the rest of the corps.

To begin with, I had never heard of guys wanting to be in the flag corps, much less actually being in one. In the band, yes; but in the flag corps? No. All the flag corps I had ever seen before had been exclusively female. Then, I couldn't help noticing Joshua's outfit had a decidedly feminine quality to it, and that he looked rather fetching in his sequined shirt and shorts. But in my heart of hearts I wasn't really surprised. Seeing him sparkling there before my eyes only confirmed what I had suspected all along. Joshua was probably gay.

Joshua had been in my second period Honors 11 class from the beginning of the year. He had been a model student, but it was hard to ignore his noticeably effeminate ways. I tried hard not to cave into the evils of stereotyping people, so I ignored as "quirkish" his flamboyant hand gestures and his hands-on-hips stances. Seeing him fitting in so comfortably with the girls of the flag corps that night, I caved right in.

In the days that followed the football game, I watched Joshua more closely to see if I had missed something. He seemed to be well-liked by the girls and guys alike. He also seemed unusually comfortable with himself, unlike other adolescents I have known who were grappling with their sexual orientation. Fortunately, his effeminate nature was tolerated at Dunbar in ways it never would have been at Wakulla County High. At Wakulla any hint of homosexuality promised threats from the rifles that rested in pickup truck gun racks. The only gays in Wakulla County closeted themselves safely away until a more generous spirit ruled the land. At Dunbar High, such behavior was openly exhibited without apparent reprisal.

Joshua was a charmer. One of the most endearing things about him to me was his fascination for my long, straight blonde hair. Of all the students I taught that year, he alone came up and actually touched my hair; "fondled" it is more like what he did. It seemed an intimate thing, and I couldn't tell if it were a black/white thing or a man/woman thing. Was he feeling the difference in our races or in our sexes?

He seemed absolutely fascinated by the texture and composition of my hair. Almost every day, I could expect to feel his long, graceful fingers rolling a few strands of my hair as he passed by on his way to his desk. I don't know if he envied me my hair or if he were repugnantly fascinated by it. I halfway expected him to approach me about hair care products.

As for intellect, Joshua was not in short supply. He read voraciously, and I often had to remind him to put away his novel and return to the classroom tasks at hand. He had a great love for romance novels. In class, however, he obsessed over Edgar Allan Poe and his stories. Joshua couldn't get enough of Poe. He wanted to know all about his sordid life and times. I was happy to assist him in his quest for knowledge.

One day after we had just started reading "The Masque of the Red Death," Joshua said, "This masque thing sounds like New Orleans and the Mardi Gras to me."

"What an excellent observation, Joshua," I replied. "It does have a carnival quality to it—covered faces, costumes, parties. The masquerade idea is rather like dressing up for the Mardi Gras, isn't it?"

"Party!" someone from the other side of the room announced, and soon others took up the chant. "Party! Party! Party!"

"All right," I said. "That's enough."

"Yes, costumes. The glorious silks and brocades—the sequins and feathers—it must be something to see and be a part of," Joshua said breathlessly as the other students slowly came to order. It was with some shame I admittedly conjured an image of him decked out for the Mardi Gras in a splendid ensemble, his flags resplendent in the raw spring breezes; the crowds wild with appreciation.

Before my daydream faded, however, Robert, who had been watching Joshua just as I had, inserted his mean-spirited commentary on the wages of sin into my class yet again.

Loudly and deliberately, Robert asked, "Ms. Webster, don't

you think homosexuality is an abomination before God like it says in the Bible?"

Before I could even open my mouth to speak, Robert began to quote Scripture in a cold and condemning voice. "It says in the Bible, 'Then the Lord rained upon Sodom and Gomorrah brimstone and fire from the Lord out of heaven; and he overthrew those cities, and all the plain, and all the inhabitants of the cities, and that which grew upon the ground.'"

An awkward silence fell across the class. I was formulating my thoughts to give a reply to this sermon when Joshua took the floor.

Without so much as a blink, he took a deep breath, looked Robert dead in the eye, and said, "Jesus said, 'Thou shalt not be as the hypocrites are: for they love to pray standing in the synagogues and in the corners of the streets, that they may be seen of men.'"

A ripple of approval seemed to move through the classroom at this final piece of Scripture. Robert was silenced, at least for the day. For the rest of our year together, I never saw or heard him publicly confront Joshua about his lifestyle again. As for me, it was clearly time to move on with my lesson. The contrasting sermonettes would have to sink in of their own accord, and I was able to sidestep this "powder keg" of a topic for another day.

LESSON 11

The Bustle in the House
The Morning after Death
Is solemnest of Industries
Enacted upon Earth—

The Sweeping up the Heart
And the putting Love away
That we shall not want to use again
Until Eternity.

"The Bustle in the House"
Emily Dickinson

I was just fifteen when I fell in love with Bill, and I was just sixteen when he moved away to Massachusetts—a good 1,300 miles from my home in Jacksonville, Florida. Never had there been such sorrow—at least never in my life. I pined and moped around for months, partly because I was truly devastated by the loss of hand-holding and making out and swimming in adoring eyes; but mostly I grieved because Bill's leaving had been like a death. He was as lost to me as if he had died. I never saw him again. Because he hadn't died, though, my grief seemed inappropriate to my parents and all my friends. No one could understand how a pretty girl like me could "hole up in her room" and not get back to the business of being young and enjoying the "best days of your life."

Once while I was babysitting, instead of dating, I happened upon an engraved card, outlined in black and stuck in the center of an encyclopedia. Upon it was written the poem, "The Bustle in the House," by Emily Dickinson, a poet from Massachusetts. The poem had been printed to mark the assassination of John F. Kennedy, a native of Massachusetts who had died as our 35th President. As my eyes moved over the words, I suddenly felt an understanding spread through me like spilled ice water seeping through clothes. Here on paper Emily had captured the sense of loss I had been feeling. Here, with simple words, images were created that I could see and feel and almost touch. An empty room-heart, a broom used to sweep up excess love that no longer had a recipient, or maybe even the pieces of a broken heart. I knew of these things; had lived with them for a very long time, and, in that moment, I awoke from my grief-stricken stupor. Poetry suddenly became accessible to me and from that day forward I have loved poetry. Even tried to write some of it now and again.

Reading that card was the first time the power of the word overwhelmed me with such force. Up until that moment, I had merely endured words as part of an educational system that said I needed to know as many words as could be stuffed into my head. Now words could make feelings transcend time. Emily, someone who had lived more than a hundred years earlier, surely must have known what I had known about losing somebody. She had captured my feeling so exactly. For that I consider her my favorite poet, and "The Bustle in the House" is my favorite poem. Emily and her poem opened my eyes to all the possibilities of metaphors and similes and images, and to her I am eternally grateful.

When it came time to begin a unit on poetic techniques for

my eleventh graders, I thought I would dig out this particular poem. My reasons were not the most original. As all adults, I figured the younger generation could learn much from my experience. For some reason, I had conveniently forgotten how my parents' stories of their youth had stopped inspiring me when I was a teenager. Still, I dusted off my favorite poem and planned to open the eyes of my standard eleventh-grade class to the joys of poetry.

"Luscious?"

"Yes, ma'am?" he answered, lifting his head up from the desk where it was resting.

Luscious, one of the project kids, had an extremely impish grin. He usually wore what some of the other teachers told me was the project kids' uniform—a white Fruit-of-the-Loom tee shirt, a pair of dark pants, and a pair of inexpensive tennis shoes. Just before school starts every fall, the WalMarts and K-Marts of the land crawl with mothers from the projects doing their back-to-school clothes shopping, and I could just see Luscious's mom in there wrestling through the shelves to get the right size pack of shirts.

But Luscious's lack of clothing style was made up for by his winning personality. He was so smooth that I'd be giving in to him before I even knew that I'd been conned. It was all right, though. He was never mean-spirited in his behavior and occasionally he'd let slip a gleam of brilliance that melted my educator's heart.

"Luscious, have you been listening to what I've been saying?"

"Sure, I have," he said, rubbing his eyes.

"And?"

"And, you never got over your first love, and you want us to write poems about it?"

The class twittered nervously, and I sighed deeply.

"Luscious, I did get over this guy eventually. I even married a totally different person, but I wasn't trying to bore you with my life story . . ."

"Too late," Luscious said.

Louder laughter followed, and I was beginning to get discouraged. "I was trying to show you how poetry can ease a burden . . ."

"Or be one," Luscious said.

Still more laughing followed.

"Are you going to let me finish any of my sentences?" I asked.

"Ah, come on, Ms. Webster," he said with his killer smile. "I was just kidding with you."

"I liked your poem, Ms. Webster," a different, soft masculine voice said. Mark, a gentle and usually quiet soul, had just spoken. I looked over at Mark and for the first time I really noticed him. His hair was cropped close and his skin had a few obvious freckles on his nose that gave him a "little boy" look. Occasionally, I'd catch him putting his head down during class, and at first, I had taken offense at it. Later on I learned from the students that Mark had gotten a part-time job with the city of Jacksonville as an auxiliary fire/rescue volunteer. That meant he often accompanied the ambulances on their way to rescues where he would actually assist in the saving of life and watch the losing of it sometimes as well. He was most ambitious about his dream of being a fireman. I had no doubt he'd make it.

Mark usually just came to class and never said a word. His volunteering a response was unexpected—like lightning on a clear Massachusetts winter day. It was almost impossible to believe.

"Thank you, Mark," I said. I waited for him to say more, but that was all I was going to get out of him for the day. I didn't want to push it. I went back to my teaching—poetic terminology and poetic techniques. Could they see the metaphor? Could they see the images? What was the rhyme scheme?

No remarkable insights emerged and we went on to read other poems in our textbook. My favorite poet and her beautiful poem receded into the shadows of my heart along with Massachusetts and Bill, and I made a mental note that maybe I should keep this poem to myself in the future. Its beauty was obviously in the eye of the beholder—me.

I did use the poem on the midterm, however. Thinking I'd be doing my students a favor, I chose it for three reasons—it was easy to understand, we had talked a great deal about it in class, and I wouldn't cause them anxiety by surprising them with a poem they had never seen before.

> In an essay of at least three paragraphs, discuss Emily Dickinson's poem, "The Bustle in the House." Don't forget to organize your essay into an introduction, body, and conclusion. You might want to discuss the poem's structure, the poem's meaning, and the poem's relationship to real life experiences. Spelling counts, so use your dictionaries.

That night, after dinner was over and all my household chores were done, I planned to finish grading the exams. Michael had retired to the couch of our great room to watch TV and I settled at the nearby dining table to work. I opened my briefcase and Luscious's paper was on top. His essay was only one, three-sentence paragraph that rambled on about how poetry can "lift you up and make you a better person."

"Well, Luscious, this is an extraordinarily awful effort," I said, as I put the "D-" in the upper left-hand corner of his paper and moved on. As I continued reading, a few papers indicated some students were totally confused. Other essays were very much on the mark. It was just that none of the writing was truly inspired. I sadly concluded, "Just because something inspires me does not necessarily mean it can inspire anyone else."

That was when I came upon Mark's paper. His was simply written. It was refreshingly clear and direct. I read the first two paragraphs about the structure and rhyme and then I came to the third.

> When my mother died last year, I was so broken-hearted that I could have died myself. I didn't. I just kept on going, but I was full of love that had no place to go because Mama

wasn't there to feel it any more. And I felt very alone. I didn't think anyone could feel as bad as I did. Emily Dickinson's poem "The Bustle in the House" really expressed what I had felt. Reading it really made me feel better. I felt better because I know now that other people have felt this way too. That is why this poem is one that I will keep in my heart forever. Thank you for teaching it to us, Mrs. Webster.

It was hard for me to read the next paper through my misted eyes.

LESSON 12

I perceived in the gloom a figure which stole from behind a clump of trees near me; I stood fixed, gazing intently; I could not be mistaken. A flash of lightning illuminated the object and discovered its shape plainly to me; its gigantic stature, and the deformity of its aspect, more hideous than belongs to humanity, instantly informed me that it was the wretch, the filthy demon to whom I had given life.

Frankenstein
Mary Shelly

A s is the case with all teachers, I was given a duty during two planning periods each week. It was easy enough to do, I suppose, but when I thought of all the many things I needed to grade and prepare for, I resented having to take time from my busy life to sit in the hall and prevent children from coming through. I suppose I should have been grateful I didn't have cafeteria duty. It was rumored that during that duty a teacher must get children to clean up after themselves. One has to get them to take their trays to the appropriate places and dump whatever trash in the cans provided. I'm not sure why teenagers feel they don't have to be tidy, courteous or do whatever is asked of them by adults. They seem to resent any interference by adults so they don't often cooperate with the cafeteria monitors.

I always went to my duty with a bit of dread. I wasn't at all sure a 5-foot 2-inch white woman would command much respect from the students at Dunbar. I wasn't sure I really respected myself, yet. Nonetheless, I had to prevent the flow of students through my assigned hall, and that was what I was going to try to do.

After the bell rang, I hurried the few straggling students out the door and closed it. Then, I positioned a chair at the wall adjacent to the door and took a seat. For the next five minutes not much happened. One girl came to the door, held a hall pass up for me to see, and I opened the door and let her by. A few minutes later a thin young man, probably a freshman, held up his pass, and I let him through.

"Today shouldn't be so bad," I said aloud to myself.

I pulled a green pen and a stack of writing assignments from my large purse and proceeded to grade them. I got through the first paragraph of the first composition when I heard a knock at the door.

"Pass?" I asked.

"I got to pee," a young girl said through the glass of the window.

"I have to see your pass."

"I don't have one."

"Well, go back to your teacher and get one."

I heard a little grumbling as she turned around and went back to where she had come. I returned to my paper. I reread the paragraph I had just finished, because I had lost its train of logic. Another knock sounded.

I looked up, and this time, there was a black woman with the same girl I had just turned away.

"Let this child pass," the woman said coldly. "She has a kidney problem."

The girl went by with a smirk on her face, and the woman

then began to scold me. "You can't prevent these children from going to the bathroom. There are laws, you know."

"But all students have to have hall passes to be in the halls between class. The principal said so. And that's all I asked for," I said defensively. I was beginning to feel an uncomfortable flush of anger rising.

"Well, I didn't have time to write her one. Okay?"

"Well, how was I supposed to know that? We were told students had to have a pass to go anywhere in this building and that's all I asked for."

"Typical," was her parting shot as she turned and huffed away.

"Well!" I thought to myself. "What was that all about?"

I knew I had followed procedure. I was doing what I was supposed to do. Why had I angered this woman so? How could I be wrong in this situation? Why did I feel as if I had done something inappropriate? I tried to put it out of my mind.

For the third time, I tried to grade the paper I had started reading earlier, and I wasn't even a sentence into it when another knock came. This student had a pass, followed by another and then another. I could see I wasn't going to get much done, so I put the compositions away, and got out a piece of scratch paper on which I began a list of things for me to do later on in the day.

I was down to the fifth item on my list—Wash load of dark clothes, esp. Michael's dress socks—when another knock came.

"I need a pass," I said pleasantly to the looming hulk of a young man who stood at my door. He was well over 6 feet tall and he must have weighed almost 300. He was tremendous.

A monstrous grimace came over his face and without any other warning, he took his tree-trunk sized arm and slammed the window as hard as I've ever heard anyone hit anything.

"Open the fuckin' door, bitch!" he bellowed.

I don't know what primal fear he stirred in me, but before I knew it, I was pressing the handle to open the door. The monster rushed past me, thankfully not taking my head with him as he stomped by, and I watched him disappear down the hall. My heart throbbed wildly, and my hand shook too much for me to write even one more thing on my list. I decided at that moment I would let anybody through who came by this door whether or not he or she had a pass. If I continued on my present course, I was either going to incur the wrath of unreasonable teachers or get killed by violent students coming through the glass. I could see I wasn't ever going to win this battle, so I just abandoned it.

Oddly enough, the young man who swore at me that fateful day was dead before the year was out. He was killed in a drive-by shooting as he stood on a street corner selling drugs in the spring. I remember that, rather than feeling vindicated in some way, I felt awful instead. Maybe if fewer of us hall monitors had not given up and given in to his demands, then he might not have gotten used to getting his way all the time. He might have found a better way to deal with the world other than slamming on doors and dealing drugs, which undoubtedly led to his young death by gunfire. And sadly, it doesn't really matter what I learned from this set of circumstances. The monster-child was dead, and hall duty never got any easier.

LESSON 13

My grandmothers were strong
They followed plows and bent to toil
They moved through fields sowing seed
They touched the earth and grain grew.
They were full of sturdiness and singing
My grandmothers were strong.

My grandmothers are full of memories
Smelling of soap and onions and wet clay
With veins rolling roughly over quick hands
They have many clean words to say
My grandmothers were strong.
Why am I not as they?

"Lineage"
Margaret Walker

Frightening—this is the only word to describe what had happened. I had been standing at my post in the hall, smiling at all the energetic faces that came my way. I didn't suspect anything was up, but as I walked into my first period class, I could tell immediately the air carried violence upon its breath. Wild animal forces were suddenly unleashed in my little classroom.

Rochelle abruptly let out a tremendous yell and ran full speed at Flosette—a huge, dark pillar of a person who had normally been quiet as a prayer. She too bellowed a furious response, and suddenly I was in the middle of a human whirlwind, the likes of which I had never seen before in my life; not even when I fought terrible battles with my brother when I was a little girl or called other little girls ugly names.

It was all I could do to keep the girls apart. Two large boys tugged the struggling Rochelle in one direction and three others were pulling the furious Flosette in the other. Profanities flew from the mouths of the combatants as Pandora's troubles had at one time flown from the box she was told not to open. Some of the spectators baited and urged the fighters on.

"Kill her, Flosette!"

"Get her! Get her!"

"Fight! Fight!"

I knew I was yelling for order at the top of my lungs, but my thin, wispy voice couldn't compete with the roar of the crowd. Control was out the window. I was aware of the incredible fury that carved a hideous face on Rochelle. I had never seen her as terrifying as this before. I was afraid even to glance at Flosette's face.

As the wave of violence swept through my room, it knocked over desks and chairs. Books and papers had been scattered everywhere. A few blows were struck with sickening accuracy. Fingernails bit into skin. The cactus dish on my desk was knocked to the floor where the pot shattered and dirt, cactus balls, and shards only added more confusion to the chaos.

I was a floundering swimmer in a hurricane sea. My head throbbed wildly. I couldn't catch my breath. I was overwhelmed by it all. I felt like the little Dutch boy holding back the crumbling dike and an overpowering sea. I let go of Rochelle, and when she stayed in place because others were restraining her frantic body, I rushed over to the intercom and pushed the panic button.

"May we help you?" a pleasant voice asked.

"Send somebody quick!"

"Excuse me?"

"Help me! There's a fight down here!"

I realized then spectators from other rooms were joining in the fracas. There seemed to be 500 people in the room. There probably weren't 50.

Suddenly, as if Moses were parting the Red Sea, the crowd split and fell silent. Sarah Weller moved commandingly into the room. Her thin, muscular arms took both girls by the scruffs of their necks and jerked them into submission. Blood glistened on Flosette's upper lip. Rochelle's weepy eye seemed already to be swollen from a direct hit, and her shirt had been torn at the shoulder. Sweat poured copiously down both faces and both girls breathed hard, panting loudly as they were escorted out of the room and down the hall to the office.

Just as quickly as it had started, it had stopped. I was amazed at how quiet it had become. My students had already begun to pull the furniture back into the proper places, righting the chairs, and someone was even sweeping up the pieces of my destroyed cactus dish. It was as if they already knew the drill. It was as if they did this clean-up operation every day.

I must have looked a sight. I sensed my hair was all a jumble and my clothes had been pulled out of place. My slip was showing at the neck of my dress and at the hemline. My pantyhose even seemed to bag at the ankles and the knees for some strange reason. I took a deep breath; then, as if I could handle anything, I tried to smooth my dress and slip back into shape as I calmly walked toward the blackboard. I tried to tuck the loose wisps of hair back behind my ears and out of my face. I worked hard at calming my considerably frayed nerves. I eventually took my place to begin the lesson.

"Open your books to page 411," I said in a shaky voice, as I wrote the page number on the board with trembling hand.

As I looked down at the page myself, I couldn't suppress my smile. Sometimes I wonder if God isn't personally watching what goes on in my life. How else could it have happened that "Lineage" was the poem for discussion today? Margaret Walker wrote about her strong grandmothers, black women who could conquer the world with their hard work and incredible strength. The fight I had just witnessed was my first real encounter with the strength and power of the descendants of those women, and I too was awed.

Five days later, both Rochelle and Flosette returned to class after their disciplinary suspensions. Their injuries were healed, and they both behaved as if nothing ferocious had ever passed between them before.

LESSON 14

"What tricks Theodore and I used to play on our Miss Wilsons and Mrs. Greys and Madame Jouberts! Mary was too sleepy to join in a plot with spirit. The best fun was Madame Joubert. Miss Wilson was a poor sickly thing, lachrymose and low-spirited: not worth the trouble of vanquishing, in short; and Mrs. Grey was coarse and insensible; no blow took effect on her. But poor Madame Joubert! I see her yet in her raging passions, when we had driven her to extremities—spilt our tea, crumbled our bread and butter, tossed our books up to the ceiling and played a charivari with the ruler and desk, the fender and fire irons.

"Theodore, do you remember those merry days?"

"Yass, to be sure I do," drawled Lord Ingram; "and the poor old stick used to cry out 'Oh, you villains childs!'—and then we sermonized her on the presumption of attempting to teach such clever blades as we were, when she herself was so ignorant."

Jane Eyre
Charlotte Bronte

The unnatural hush that had fallen over the room should have given their scheme away. They thought they were being so clever. Thought I wouldn't see the rubber tarantula's leg sticking out of my center desk drawer. But I was on to their little trick and did NOT act surprised when I opened the drawer and the hideous monster dropped into my lap.

"My, my, what have we here?" I said, lifting the thing up in the air so all the students and tricksters could see I wasn't afraid.

A collective sigh of exasperation moved through the room and I went on with the lesson.

"Jane Eyre was one of my favorite literary characters when I was a young girl. I used to read about her at least once a year."

"Why would anyone want to do that?" I heard Roscoe say to his neighbors.

"Well, for one reason, I enjoyed reading about how Jane overcame terrible obstacles to find her way in the world. She is the first liberated woman in English literature, you know. Before Jane, women characters seemed to be mostly the prizes men fought over, and they weren't nearly as interesting as the men were. Jane, however . . ."

"Hey, what about Hester in . . . what's that book called?" someone asked.

"The book is called *The Scarlet Letter* and it's Hester Prynne. Anyway, she is an American character. We are studying British literature in this class."

"Humph," Roscoe said. "Well, what about how boring the writing is? I mean, it takes these guys forever to say something very simple."

"You know, for the first time, Roscoe, you and I agree. Jane Eyre is written in very 'ornate' language. It is almost 'verbose.' Now, there are two new words you need to add to your vocabulary list."

"Way to go, Roscoe!" Thomas, a short and puny little kid, said as he gave Roscoe a swift punch in the arm.

I rose and turned to go to the board, when I saw three rubber cockroaches and two giant rubber flies lining the chalk tray.

"My, my. What have we here?" I said to myself as I carefully picked up each creature and then dropped each very deliberately into the trash can nearby. Another exasperated sigh moved across the room. Then I returned to my place at the board.

"O-r-n-a-t-e," I spelled with the squeaky chalk that I had to use since the overhead permanently gave up the ghost about a week earlier. "It means 'overly fancy.' Look up a more complete definition for the test Friday.

"V-e-r-b-o-s-e," my chalk squeaked. "This means 'wordy.'"

As the dutiful students wrote these words in their vocabulary notebooks and the lazy ones just watched, I moved around to the front of my desk so I could more easily talk about the chapter they had had to read for homework. There at my feet was a dead rubber rat.

"Good heavens! We are going to have to get the exterminator out here soon!" I said loudly and deliberately.

Another trick foiled. I was wonderful as I took the rubber critter to the trashcan, and dramatically dropped him in. Without missing a step, I asked Shamika, "Why do you suppose Ms. Bronte wrote in so 'ornate' and 'verbose' a style?"

Shamika, a graceful milk-chocolate-brown beauty, grew thoughtful and finally concluded, "People just talked like that back in those days?"

"I would think they might," I agreed. "They didn't have television or movies back then, so some of their major pastimes would be conversation and reading. Both conversation and reading involve the use of many words. Since it was all they had to do for fun, it stands to reason their language would be more ornate."

"I bet that wasn't all they had to do for fun," Roscoe smirked to his pal sitting next to him.

Snickers filled the room.

"You know what I am talking about, Roscoe," I said.

I was about to continue, when suddenly a real live spider

wobbled his way into the center of the room for all the world to see. It was a daddy-long-legs and whether he had just wandered in from outside or someone had just released him from a jar into the room, I don't know. I was, at that moment, sorely tested. What was I going to do with a real live critter? How would I successfully deal with this unanticipated trick?

Hoping nobody was noticing, I took a deep breath, went over to the spider and carefully picked him up by one of his gossamer legs. He sort of hung there stupidly and I, hoping he wouldn't reach his other legs around and get on me, calmly walked out of the classroom, down the hall and out of the building where I released the little fellow in the straw-like winter grass. He hurried away and I shivered slightly at the thought of what I had just done. I took another deep breath and returned to my classroom.

Pandemonium ruled as I reentered my door.

"What is going on here?" I scolded. "Can't I leave this room for even five seconds without you all going berserk?"

"Ms. Webster, you touched it!" Shamika squealed. "You actually touched it!"

"Ew!" Roscoe said loudly. "How could you do that?"

"It's simple," I said, "I just picked him up by one of his little legs . . ."

"Stop! Stop! I can't stand it!" Shamika said, covering her ears as if I were scraping my fingernails down the chalkboard or something equally nerve-racking.

"Class, it was just a little spider."

"But you touched it!" Shamika squealed again.

"Why didn't you just step on it?" Roscoe asked, a look of incredulity on his face.

"I don't kill spiders," I said.

"Why not?"

"Because everyone knows it's bad luck to kill spiders."

"It is?" several students said almost in unison, their eyes wide with what looked like terror.

"That's what my grandmother always used to tell me," I said.

"Besides, spiders eat mosquitoes and flies. They are good for the ecology. Now, let's get back to the novel, *Jane Eyre.*"

I don't really know what sociological event happened that day in my class, but I sensed that somehow I had acquired a new, almost superior status after I touched the spider. It was as if I had proved to the world I could do anything; there was nothing I couldn't do.

A few weeks later during my planning period, the librarian, an imposing woman who had not shown me the slightest courtesy and even seemed to dislike me a great deal, came to my room and asked if I would come and remove a dead mouse from under her desk. Apparently, the custodian couldn't get to it for a while, and she had heard I was "brave about these sorts of things."

I went with her to the library and bravely whooshed the little gray body onto a piece of cardboard with another piece of cardboard. I then deposited the animal into the nearest receptacle and that was that. Oddly enough, cheers suddenly filled the room. Others had been watching from the door of the room and I became a heroine. I was amazed, and the librarian cannot do enough for me now. She became my friend for life.

Never in all my dreams would I have thought myself so brave. I have to turn my head when they show operations on the television, and when I take my cat, Humphrey, to the vet I cannot watch as they give him his shots. Even so, to the population at Dunbar I was "something else," and all because it was important that I not lose face in front of my students.

LESSON 15

The time you won your town the race,
We chaired you through the market place;
Man and boy stood cheering by,
And home we brought you shoulder high.

Today, the road all runners come,
Shoulder high we bring you home,
And set you at your threshold down,
Townsman of a stiller town.

Smart lad, to slip betimes away
From fields of glory does not stay
And early though the laurel grows
It withers quicker than the rose . . . .

"To An Athlete Dying Young"
A. E. Houseman

Although Shermon was not a student of mine, he was a friend to everyone at the school, it seemed. His death at a Friday night football game cast a pall over the entire school and ultimately the entire year. The shooting occurred in the parking lot, not twenty minutes after the Vikings had routed the Tigers of Etonville High, one of the school's biggest rivals. Shermon, one of the football players, and his girlfriend had met after the game in the parking lot where some street hoodlums who had crashed the gates earlier had been harassing her. He had tried futilely to protect his girlfriend from their advances when one of the criminals pulled out a gun and shot Shermon in the head. He died where he fell, his life snuffed out quickly as the bullet passed through his brain.

I had already left the stadium and was on the highway home when the shooting occurred. I can only imagine the sheer panic that swept through the remaining crowd. Or the terror and hurt of the girlfriend as she watched the person she loved destroyed. Or the horror of the coaches and staff who worked diligently over a body they had to know was dead already, and I can only imagine the unthinkable pain the family and close friends felt when they got the news of Shermon's death.

All the next week, I watched grief live itself out at Dunbar. I had never seen so many people "fall out" in my life. Girls were swooning, two and three a class period, in various parts of the school, and having to be carried to the front office to compose themselves. Boys didn't cry that I could see, but their faces were unusually stern. The lively rhythm of the school had been interrupted, and students dragged quietly and slowly through their day.

Often, I would see guys stoically supporting the weeping, then fainting, girls in an often grotesque drama that unfolded before my eyes. It reminded me of the tragic death by suicide of a young man in my senior year of high school.

Joey, a rather distant acquaintance of mine, had marched out to the pitcher's mound during a ball game, put a gun in his mouth and pulled the trigger. I read about it in the paper the next day and went violently cold and clammy. All sorts of thoughts ran through my mind—foolish thoughts about how maybe I could have prevented it had I known of his sorrow. Maybe I could have helped him through a tough time by just smiling at him or engaging him in conversation. What I think I must have been feeling was extreme guilt—guilt that I was still alive—that it was he and not I who had died.

When I got to school the first day after Joey's death, I felt as if I had slipped into another dimension. Everybody was red-eyed and seemed to be moving in a slow-motion pantomime. It was as if the air had grown incredibly thick, like water. I felt as if I were in a Jacques Cousteau film, making my way in an undersea world like one of a school of fish. Nothing really penetrated my senses that day. I was safely insulated from the reality of death in my new world.

Two weeks later, though, I broke down in heavy sobs in the middle of my biology class when we were dissecting fetal pigs. It took my peers and ME by surprise. The teacher escorted me to the office where I called my mother, and she came and took me home. There I cried all the rest of the day. Then, after that afternoon's episode, I was fine. It is strange how differently humans react to the death of another human being.

When grief is as overwhelming as it was at Dunbar High that week, the only thing I as a teacher could do was to allow students to ventilate their feelings. That's exactly what I did, and, believe me, they really ventilated. There were many testimonials given in my classes about how wonderful and kind Shermon was.

Marvelette had tears in her eyes as she spoke of the tragedy. "I could see the little bullet coming out of Shermon's head as he laid there all dead and still in a big pool of blood." She closed her eyes hard and the tears ran down her cheeks. "Oh, God, there was so much blood."

"Shermon was one of my very best friends," Percy said of his teammate to my fourth-period students. "He and I used to go to American Beach and pick up girls. He'd come and get me in that raggedy old car of his, and we'd just cruise. He even taught me about how to get girls to like me."

I braced myself for an insult like, "Girls don't like you, Percy." But, thankfully, it didn't come. I guess there are just some times when all joking is put aside and life gets unbearably heavy. Percy put his head down on the top of the desk where he appeared to sleep for the rest of the class. I left him alone until the end of the class, when I could no longer resist going to his desk and putting a reassuring hand on his shoulder. The bell rang and, as Percy got up to leave, he averted his face and hurried out of the room.

Shermon's funeral was on Thursday, an agonizing day. Those of us who did not go to the New Bethel AME Church stayed behind at school to cover classes for Shermon's teachers and friends. The school building was almost empty. I had only seven students in my fifth-period class since everyone else had gone to the church to say their goodbyes.

When Mr. Mattox, who had been Shermon's ninth-grade social studies teacher, got on the intercom during the funeral hour to eulogize Shermon, his voice wavered, and he choked twice during his speech.

"Shermon was more than just a football player. He was a football lover, and he wanted to share his love of the sport with others. I remember one summer when he drove little kids from the projects to the rag-tag games across town so they could take part in the sport. He even spent his own money on some of the kids so they could get shoes to play. And he was always showing the little ones how to kick and pass the ball. He was a kind . . . a kind, gentle man; the kind that the world needs a lot more of, and I am so dreadfully sorry he will not live to recognize his own value to his community . . ." Mr. Mattox was so overcome with emotion that he had to stop. The intercom went silent.

I bowed my head, covered my face with my hands, and let the tears slip softly from my eyes along with the rest of my students. We mourned together, each in our own way, the tragic loss of one of our finest.

DECEMBER

LESSON 16

"I have always thought a body would have to be sick and dying before they saw the Lord. And I imagined that when He came it would be like looking at the Baptist window: pretty as colored glass with the sun pouring through, such a shine you don't know it's getting dark. And it has been a comfort: to think of that shine taking away all the spooky feeling. But I'll wager it never happens. I'll wager at the very end a body realizes that the Lord has already shown Himself . . . ."

"A Christmas Memory"
Truman Capote

In Jacksonville, Florida, every year for quite some time, the *Florida Times-Union*, our only newspaper, sponsors a Christmas short story contest. In a burst of first-year enthusiasm, I decided it would be a tremendously beneficial activity to have all my students enter the contest. Of course, this would mean the contest sponsors would be inundated with entries, especially if other teachers in the area had the same bright idea. But I felt that even if that happened to the paper, they couldn't complain if the quality of the work was high. Besides, that was their problem. If they wanted to limit the participation, then it was up to them to worry with that.

I started the project by having my students read classic Christmas stories, like "A Christmas Memory" by Truman Capote and "A Christmas Carol" by Charles Dickens. Then we spent the next few days sharing as many Christmas memories as we could remember.

Soon our mouths watered at the memory-smell of cookies baking and honeyed hams in the oven. Soon our eyes sparkled with memories of dazzling lights that dotted the scenery of Jacksonville neighborhoods. Our ears soon rang with the sound of Salvation Army bells and the Christmas carols being played on radios and television. Soon, no one remembered this was a "dumb idea" and "maybe this assignment wasn't so crazy after all." By the end of the project, we all looked forward to holidays to bring us a new set of memories to be catalogued in our hearts.

The Monday after Thanksgiving, the final drafts of their stories were due. As was my custom, I had washed my dinner dishes that night, then found my quiet grading spot and settled in for a long winter's read. A coffee cup steamed at my side and Humphrey, in all his furry glory, purred in my lap.

I had several favorite stories. There was Vermellia's about how she disobeyed her mother's warning not to go into the living room Christmas Eve or Santa Claus might not come. Little did she know she had left little-girl footprints in the freshly vacuumed carpet her mother could easily detect. They led her mother straight to the closet where Vermellia hid.

There was Andrew's story about trying to hide a pecan pie behind his back only to "drop it, splat, face down on his mama's newly cleaned linoleum."

Then I chuckled when I read Juanita's story about her little brother, Chester, who had been playing football in the house when he kicked the ball into the greens pot cooking on the stove. The pot was so high up and so hot that he had to leave the ball where it landed. His grandmother almost had a heart attack when the ball exploded sometime later, splattering greens over all the kitchen walls. "Of course, no one knew how the ball got there."

My favorite story belonged to Luscious. Luscious's greatest talent was telling funny stories and entertaining the rest of the students, sometimes to the detriment of my lesson. His voice was what drew people to him. It was most distinctive, and as I read each word of his story, I could hear his deep, sonorous voice reading it to me.

> The best Christmas memory I have is not really my memory. It is a story my Grandfather Johnston used to tell before he died. Long ago, back in the '50s, my grandfather scrimped and saved every nickel and penny he could get. Finally, he had enough to buy a car, not a brand new car, but one that was new to his family. He went into town from the farm that he lived on, and on Christmas Eve he came driving down the dirt road in the family's Christmas present—a black 1951 Ford.

> The entire family of cousins and brothers and sisters piled into the Ford all excited and thrilled. Arms, elbows and knees stuck out everywhere. Even Great-Grandmother Jesse waddled out of the house on her cane and got in the back seat for the first ride. Everyone was so happy. Grandfather Johnston was especially happy and in a celebrating mood. He got out a chaw of tobacco and chewed.

> They had driven a bunch of miles enjoying the beautiful Mandarin scenery. The low, moss-covered branches and horse-filled fields whizzed past the windows as the family sang Christmas songs. Soon it was time for Grandfather Johnston to spit. He let loose out his window and no sooner than his tobacco had hit the breeze than it swung back in the back seat window and hit Great-Grandmother Jesse square in the face.

Well, she starts hollering and screaming as the nasty stuff rolls all down her face. Then she starts hitting her son with her cane on the top of his head. This makes him start hollering and he runs off the road. Everybody is screaming and hollering. In all the noise the big old Ford jumps off the road, down a bank, and up against a tree stump that's in the tall grass. The front end of the car was all crinkled and bent, but no one was hurt. Except maybe for Grandfather Johnston's pride and the top of his head.

I put my stack of papers down and laughed until I scared Humphrey out of my lap and under the sofa. Michael emerged from the bedroom to see what was going on. I could just see all those folks crammed into a car with a screaming great-grandmother and an airborne Ford. It made me think of the family stories my relatives tell each wedding, funeral, Fourth of July, or Christmas gathering. We tell them all, over and over again. And as I saw smiling white faces of my family in my mind, their faces changed; they became the smiling brown faces of my students and their families. It was then I realized the races are much closer than one could ever imagine. Maybe cities across the land could enjoy better race relations if everyone sat down and told Grandfather Johnston or exploding greens stories.

Perhaps then the Lord would make Himself known to all people and peace on earth would become reality.

LESSON 17

Lives of great men shall remind us
We can make our lives sublime,
And, departing, leave behind us
Footprints in the sands of time;

"A Psalm of Life"
Henry Wadsworth Longfellow

Tyrone was cool. As one student once put it during a similes exercise we were writing, Tyrone was as cool as "a sip of ice tea on a hot summer's day." He was, too. His appropriately muscular frame swaggered into my class every day wearing the latest fashions and jewelry. He almost held court as the girls flocked around his seat to chit-chat and flirt before the lesson began.

Tyrone was definitely going to college, and not on a football scholarship, but on an academic one. He was well-read and savvy without being pompous. I loved having him in class. He didn't have to say much to sway public opinion, but when some students said a story was stupid or dumb, he would often come to my rescue and defend my choice of material by simply saying he liked it. The complaining almost instantly stopped.

Tyrone started showing up in the poetry society's meeting in the library, just to watch and listen at first. He never even spoke a word for the first two sessions he attended. Then, one session he showed up with an anthology of African-American poems.

"What a great turn-out!" I said, getting the session underway. "Who wants to start us off?"

"I do," Tyrone said softly, and with great deliberateness in his motions, he stepped to the podium to begin his reading. He opened the book, paused to look at the audience, and then began to read a set of poems by Imamu Amiri Baraka. Silence fell over the group as if a prayer were being spoken. When Tyrone finally came to the powerful end, Yasmina, who had become quite a regular poetry society member, broke the silence with, "That was really nice. Read another."

He smiled and carefully pulled a tattered notebook from his book bag. He then began to read one of his own excellent poems. All the students in the audience appeared to be awe-struck by his performance and his talent. If I hadn't happened to glance in her direction, I might have missed the fact that Rochelle appeared to be angry. She was beginning to act in an agitated manner, and then, as if she had had her fill of something distasteful, she stormed out of the library. Fortunately, I was one of only a few people who noticed her departure at all.

For the rest of the session, Tyrone entertained the group with poem after poem of his own. He could rap out his poems as perfectly as any person I had ever heard. Of course, I was probably not the best judge of rap, but the group of students in the audience was. They loved Tyrone's work. He had the gift.

Unlike many of his "wanna-be-rapper" friends, he seemed to be as concerned for the meaning of his words as he was for the rhyme and rhythm. That made him different from his peers. Most high school kids are untidy with their verse. They'll stick in any number of beats to the measure when they create, but not Tyrone.

Once he had set the cadence, be it iambs or trochees, he never wavered from the beat and never put in even one too many syllables. His words were precise and meaningful, and he wasn't afraid to tell the sad stories to which he had been witness. He peppered his work with appropriate profanities and graphic details, sometimes making me cringe, hoping no officials were around to object. Tyrone's poetry could be quite unsettling at times.

Some of the older black teachers who had wandered over to see what was going on seemed the most unsettled by his work. When Tyrone had finished one of his poems, a gym teacher there said, "That's a pretty bleak picture you're painting of this community, Son. Why don't you write more about the good things our people can do and less about the hard life we are trying to escape?"

"I write it like I see it," Tyrone answered. And I was proud he stood up for his art. I didn't want to lose Tyrone, the poet. I didn't want him to sugar-coat his poetry. Poetry didn't have to be pretty or about love or trees or flowers. It could be about "life's futility" and "broken windows in crack houses" and "dying drunks puking in the alley." All that poetry ever has to be is real, and Tyrone had realness down pat.

When the poetry meeting was over and I was going back to my room, I saw Rochelle, sitting dejectedly on the floor outside my room.

"I saw you leave before the meeting was over, Rochelle. Was it something I said?"

"I just couldn't listen to that Tyrone guy any more. He was acting like he knew all there was to know about being a poet and he didn't know shit."

"Rochelle," I said, amazed at her vehement attitude. "Tyrone is a great poet. He's very talented, and I'm going to help him get some of his work out there, if I can."

"Well, I think he stank!"

"We each have our own opinions," I said, my door unlocked by now.

"Mrs. Webster, which of us is better?"

"What are you talking about?"

"Which of us is a better poet?"

I could see she was deeply troubled about something, and Tyrone really threatened her position in the poetry group. I suppose since she had been the group's darling for such a long time this newcomer was unsettling to her. It was like having a new baby brother brought home to a family you thought was just fine as it was.

"Neither one of you is better. There is no such thing as a best poet, anyway," I said, setting up for my next class. "Poetry shouldn't be a competition. It should just be a part of our lives that helps us fill in the gaps and helps us cope with the troubles we have."

Her hard, angry face seemed to soften a bit. "So you still think I'm pretty good?"

"Of course. As long as you are writing about real things and real feelings, poetry can be more than art. Take the Japanese. I read somewhere they write poems all through their lives. There was this one Japanese man I read about who was on a jetliner that was crashing, and as the plane was going down, he took what time was left of his life to write his death poem. Can you imagine such a thing? That blew me away when I read about it. That's when I decided poetry needs to be more a part of everyone's life in America, too."

The bell had rung and students were beginning to crowd our conversation as they filed into my classroom. Rochelle was infinitely calmer than when I first encountered her in the hall.

"Go on to your next class, Rochelle. Then write me a great poem tonight about what you are feeling, okay?"

"Okay," she smiled, and she seemed to go happily into a world that needed more poems.

LESSON 18

"Jesus wept."

The Bible
King James Version

I am not sure why it was that it fell to me, but I was always the cry-baby of the family. From my first memory—a dark, spooky night at my grandparents' house when my grandfather's snoring had awakened me and frightened me into hysterical weeping—to my junior prom when I spilled punch on my expensive, baby-blue formal, I have teared up at the least little thing. My father would often tell me to cut it out or he would actually give me something to cry about, but that only seemed to make the tears flow more. My mother would scold me that boys don't like weepy girls since it does terrible things to a woman's face. And, still, I cried. When I was in elementary school, I was the brunt of many jokes by mean-spirited little boys whose mission in life, it seemed, was to see who could get me going first. Johnny Mariani was the most successful at it. It got to the point where all he had to do was look at me cross-eyed, and I'd be a mass of sobs.

Later, in high school, my girl friends would giggle and point at me all the time. "There she goes again!" they'd say when they would catch my sniffling in a movie theater or see me becoming emotional watching an old blind man begging on the corner. "You are such a weenie!" they would tell me and laugh.

Eventually my family, my friends and I all resigned ourselves to the fact that I was an unusually sensitive soul and not much was going to change that reality. Ever since, I have tried to channel the flood of tears within me. One step that I took was to become an English major so that I could hopefully find solace and refuge behind the covers of books. Of course, all the pieces of literature that I found to have any meaning or value were the pieces that made me tear-up. As a matter of fact, I have used the four-hankie measure for the quality of my books, just as movie critics use stars or popcorn boxes. For instance, *Mrs. Mike*, one of my favorite books as an adolescent, was a three-and-a-half hankie book. It didn't quite qualify as a four-hankie book the way *Jane Eyre* or *Wuthering Heights* had, but it had sufficient cry-power to rank up there with the classics.

For the longest time I thought I was the only person in the whole world to have this problem, but as I grew older and broadened my experience base, I realized that many others in this world are in a constant battle with their emotions. Perhaps it was just that I was less fortunate in finding ways to conceal my feelings. Perhaps my head could not turn fast enough for tears to escape detection, or maybe my hand was not as quick as others in wiping the tears from the cheeks.

One day after a lively discussion in second period about subject-verb agreement, I noticed that Leanne, my particular favorite, did not sit in her usual seat. Instead she sat in an empty desk in the far corner of the classroom that day, and she was visibly distraught.

No one but me could see her tears because all the students were facing forward. She worked hard at catching each tear before it fell on her papers or book, and soon she simply put her head down and covered her face so no one could see, including me. I waited until after the bell had rung. When the class was finally empty of all students but Leanne, I walked over to her desk and sat down in the seat across from her. She still had her head down on her desk, and I was not sure she was aware that I was even there.

"Is there anything I can do?" I finally asked. I didn't want to pry.

She shook her head no.

"Shall I help you to the office? Or can I get you something to drink?" I remembered how Lydia's Coke had comforted me so much on that first day of school.

Again Leanne shook her head.

I took a deep breath. "Sometimes," I said, "it helps to talk about things." Since I had a whole planning period ahead of me, I knew that I could devote at least an hour to helping her if she needed it.

"I don't think talking is going to help this problem," she finally responded, as she raised her head and revealed a swollen, tear-stained face. "Some things just can't be helped."

Her appearance touched a part of my heart where my tears live, and I could feel a good cry coming on as I looked at her sorrowful face. "Maybe talking won't change things, but it might make things more bearable."

"Not this thing," she said with a great sob.

Tears now filled my eyes, so I rushed to my desk and brought us both back the tissue box. She took three and I took two. We both dabbed our eyes.

"Leanne, I really don't know how to help you unless you tell me what's bothering you."

"All right," she said in almost a challenging way. "I'm pregnant."

My tears almost instantly dried up and a lump came to my throat so I could hardly speak. I had been hoping she was just upset over not passing a test or being stood up for a lunch date. I had hoped that she was distraught over losing an important assignment or a bracelet. Pregnancy was a problem that was obviously trickier. And I wasn't at all sure I was up to the challenges a discussion about it would present.

"I see," I said in a very soft voice.

"And to top it all off," she continued, "I'm not sure who the father is."

I swallowed hard. Her problem was getting bigger and more complex with each sentence she uttered. I was hoping that she didn't need to tell me more.

"I see," I said once more.

"My only choice is to have an abortion," she said as I listened. "I haven't got the nerve to let these guys know I've been with both of them in the same month. And my mother would absolutely kill me if she even knew I was with either of them. And after all she's been through with me, how can I face her? She'll be crushed!"

I nodded sympathetically.

"And what would God think if I aborted this baby He gave me? Oh, I wish I could go back in time just a few weeks." She began to sob at this point and I could only touch her shoulder with a reassuring hand.

Finally, when the tears subsided, I said, "Leanne, are you absolutely sure you're pregnant? I mean, have you been to a doctor?"

"Not yet," she said, "but I'm two weeks late and I'm just like clockwork, if you know what I mean."

I nodded some more. "Well, if I were you, I would get to my doctor this very afternoon. You may be worried over nothing. Women can be late for a lot of reasons, even very regular women. If the doctor says you're pregnant, THEN you start to worry and start considering options."

Leanne had by this time calmed down considerably. She blew her nose loudly and then looked me directly in the eye.

"You may be right, Miss Webster. I could just be late. Until I know for sure that I am pregnant, why should I get all upset?"

"That's right," I said, with as reassuring a smile as I could muster.

"Then, that's what I'll do. I'm going straight to the clinic right now."

She gathered her books and papers together and grabbed her purse. As she started out the door, she turned and, smiling, said, "Thanks."

"Don't mention it."

In the silence that followed, I sat in the back of my classroom and let my tired mind wander. How is it that people get themselves into such predicaments, I thought. I tried to imagine being all of fifteen or sixteen and wondering if I were pregnant and, if I were, who the father might be. And it was then that I realized what a weenie I really was. The severity of the things over which I cry is not even close to what some people have to endure.

When Leanne entered my classroom the next day, she was all smiles. She hurried over to me and hugged me around the neck. "I'm not!" she announced proudly. "Thank you, thank you, thank you!" she sang.

"I'm so glad!" I said as I delighted in her joy.

"The test I took yesterday came back negative and then my 'little friend' came last night."

"Well, I hope this means you'll be a little more careful in the future?"

"Oh, yes, ma'am!" she said with a laugh. "I got me some medication, if you know what I mean."

Here she gave me a little wink. I smiled even though I was saddened to realize how "grown" this young girl was when she should be worrying mostly about proms and football games instead of who might be her baby's daddy.

"Leanne, I know I'm not your mother, and I may not have a right to be saying these things to you, but you really need to slow down a bit as well, don't you think? I mean, there are other things to worry about besides what we talked about. You really do owe it to your unborn children to want them desperately. And your life will go so much more smoothly if you postpone families until you're an adult. And there is the matter of the diseases you can get. I'd be devastated for you to get something bad like AIDS."

"I hear what you're saying," she assured me as she hugged me, then bounced joyfully to her desk.

I felt my heart tremble as I watched her go, still oblivious to the gravity of life's unseen tragedies that lurk around every corner. I could only pray that she would take my advice to heart. I hoped I had done enough.

JANUARY

LESSON 19

Mistah Kurtz—he dead.
A penny for the Old Guy.

I

We are the hollow men
We are the stuffed men
Leaning together
Headpiece filled with straw. Alas!
Our dried voices, when
We whisper together
Are quiet and meaningless
As wind in dry grass
Or rats' feet over broken glass
In our dry cellar.

"The Hollow Men"
T. S. Eliot

Every day as I drove to work, I was amazed by the number of human beings who are up, dressed, and ready for the day at the ungodly hour of 6:10 in the morning. Even then the traffic was formidable, and if I'd missed the appropriate "window for launch" or if there were an accident on any one of the city's four major downtown bridges, I was sure to be late.

I wasn't aware of it at first, but it became apparent to me as the school year wore on there was an extremely impoverished neighborhood I had to pass through every day to get to Dunbar. On one corner of that neighborhood, next to a little grocery store, a group of dark men always stood around. In the fall they were dressed in light clothes. In the winter they wore heavy jackets and stood around a large oil drum with a fire burning in it. In the spring, I assumed they would again be back in their lighter clothes.

When I told my husband about these men, he said he thought they were day laborers. They would wait at certain corners of the city for the building contractors to come by in trucks and hire a few at low hourly wages, just for the day. It made me sad to think about it. I thought of all the jokes I'd heard about people on welfare, and then I thought of these men who seemed to be hungry for work. So hungry for it that they'd awake before the sun and stand out in the elements waiting for opportunity. It didn't seem all that lazy to me. But then I overheard some of the children talking about this corner as being a corner of known drug dealers. These guys might not be as noble as I thought. They might just be hanging around waiting for little kids to pass by so they could corrupt the children and make their ill-gotten money off the innocent.

I never passed that corner since without trying to scrutinize the faces of the men, trying to see either evil or industry. What can looks tell you, though? Some days I did indeed see drug dealers, hulking monsters trying to snare our children into the dens of iniquity. Other times, depending on my mood, I saw men looking for opportunity—black Horatio Algers in need of just one small break to make it big. Either perception was possible.

Shamika, a beautiful young woman in my sixth-period class, apparently was as confused about such things as I. It was rumored she dated a young Harry Belafonte look-alike who was a notorious drug dealer. I often wondered what a drug dealer would want with a high school girl, but Shamika was, after all, a striking beauty. Her hair was always arranged in attractive styles—from cornrows to long straight manes. Her clothes were quite striking, not necessarily because of their stylishness, but because of how well they accentuated her body parts. Occasionally she sported a wash-off tattoo prominently displayed on her bosom, which some of the students commented on loudly enough to be heard at the front of the classroom. Shamika seemed oblivious to the criticism that floated around her and went on about her studies as if she were wearing a nun's habit.

Most of the guys couldn't keep their eyes off her. Whenever she was in the classroom, they watched her, but these same guys also knew who she was connected to and knew not to touch. They simply worshiped her from afar.

The girls in the classroom just barely tolerated Shamika's beautiful presence. She wasn't close to anyone I could see, but no one ever put her in her place even when she bubbled over with exuberance. Shamika was very lively and friendly. She always had something to contribute to the class discussions of the stories, and she wasn't afraid to be wrong either. She could take criticism much better than I could.

"I know enough to know I don't want to be and won't be poor if I can help it," she announced to the class one day.

"We can tell," Arthina, the class conscience, said.

"Now, just what are you trying to say to me, Arthina?" Shamika asked, not willing to ignore the insult.

"Well," Arthina said a bit more softly, "what I'm saying is you don't strike me as the type to let poverty enter into your doorway."

"Humph," Shamika said. "You're just jealous."

"Of what?"

"Of what I have."

"Which is?"

"A fine bootie and a loving man."

At this the class broke into the usual "ooo's" and "ahhh's." A nervous kind of laughter went through the crowd—the kind that recognized truth in jesting.

"Well, you best watch that your man don't love you to death," Arthina said.

"And what do you mean by that?" Shamika said, swinging around to face Arthina this time.

"Drug dealing is what I mean. You're as likely to be with him when a bad deal goes down as not."

"That's a lie. Reggie does not deal drugs!"

"Now, there's the lie."

"You had best keep your thoughts to yourself then." Shamika turned back around and crossed her arms across her chest.

"Well, that is the only way you're going to get out of your hell-hole-of-a-life. By not hanging on to some guy that's sucking his own people dry with drugs so he can dress you up to be prettier than the rest of us," Arthina said.

"You're just jealous," she repeated solemnly, and the conversation died right there.

A few weeks later, I noticed Shamika hadn't been to class in quite a while. It had been well over a week since I had heard her friendly voice or seen her cheerful face. On that Friday as I was taking roll, I asked the class if anyone knew where she'd been.

There was a dreadful silence until Roscoe finally got up the nerve to speak.

"Don't you read the newspapers, Ms. Webster? That shooting on the Southside was Shamika's boyfriend. It was a bad drug deal, I guess, 'cause he and another guy were shot dead in the head while they were sitting in Shamika's parents' parking lot."

"Oh, my God," I whispered. "Is Shamika okay?"

"Yeah," Arthina said. "He had just dropped her off for the night, so she was inside her house when it happened. She wasn't hurt, but she did see it all come down from her bedroom window."

"How is she doing?"

"As well as can be expected," Arthina said solemnly.

"But what else could you expect to happen when you hang around people like Reggie?" Roscoe asked the question I suppose we were all thinking.

I sorrowfully shook my head. It was, after all, the only logical conclusion to Shamika's love affair. It still made me sad. It made us all sad.

We tried to reach out to Shamika. Just before the funeral, we had all signed a sympathy card and mailed it to her. I even had tried to call her house, but the number I had been given only reached a disconnected phone.

The saddest part came when we had to see the change in Shamika when she finally returned to class the following week. She was wearing a black trench coat and sunglasses, and she had wrapped herself in a shroud of silence that hardly lifted for the rest of the year.

"How are you doing?" I asked in my kindest voice when I finally had a chance to talk to her alone.

"I'll make it okay," she said softly.

I was sure she would make it. It was just going to be a little harder than she had planned.

LESSON 20

Francisco: Stand ho! Who is there?

Hamlet, Act I, Scene 1
William Shakespeare

"I didn't know Shakespeare was so nasty, man!" Mario said loudly.

Along with much chuckling, there were so many "Ho's" were being repeated around the rows, that you'd have thought Santa was in our midst.

"I'm not sure I follow you," I said.

"Stand HO?" Mario said emphatically, I suppose so that I could understand his point.

"Well, what about 'Stand ho?'" The class again fell laughing, and it took several minutes for the crowd to calm itself down.

"Now, Mrs. Webster, do you mean to tell us you don't know what a 'ho' is?" Percy said with a slight smile on his lips.

Suddenly, the light went on in my head and I understood. "Ho" meant "whore." Okay, okay. I got it now, and I probably turned red since I could feel the heat rush through my face. My class seemed to laugh even more when that happened. And it was pretty funny, when I actually thought about it. I guess having just finished my last college Shakespeare course a scant twelve months earlier, I wasn't expecting this particular and unintentional pun on Shakespeare's part; but I am sure "Willie" would have loved this verbal accident better than the kids. If he had had any idea the language would have changed so much with the passage of time, he probably would have written this scene far more enigmatically and exploited this double entendre for all it was worth. Then for centuries scholars would be able to analyze the syntax and connotation of the scene so no one would be able to enjoy it.

"All right, all right," I finally said out loud. "I get it, and you're right. It is very funny. Ha. Ha. But you need to know that in Shakespeare's day the word 'ho' meant something entirely different. It was a kind of greeting or battle cry like 'Tally Ho.'"

This explanation didn't seem to lower the mirth level of the class. It seemed to get the students really laughing now.

"Tally, ho?" Mario asked gleefully. "Isn't that what the pimp asks his girls to do when they bring him the money?"

The class erupted all over again, and this time I couldn't help joining in.

"Hey, Ho!" Mario said to his female neighbor, who promptly punched him in the arm.

"Mario," I said after thinking for a few moments and waiting for the class to come to some kind of order, "Shakespeare doesn't have to skirt around the subject. When he wants to say 'whore,' he'll just say it."

The room fell silent as if a bomb had just been dropped and all life forms had been extinguished. I looked around cautiously as the awkward silence stretched itself out for a considerable time.

Finally, Tamara's lone condescending voice said, "Ooooo, Ms. Webster talking like that. Um hm hm!"

"Well, Shakespeare would have," I defended myself. "As a matter of fact he actually does." I could hear a few sets of teeth being sucked in disbelief.

"Anyway, let's proceed. Avery, would you please take up with Horatio's line?"

Students who were playing the different roles read on in the scene. They read about the ghost of Hamlet's father, and they read how Hamlet confronts the ghost and learns of the murder of his father at the hands of Hamlet's uncle. We then learned that Hamlet makes his friends swear not to reveal what they have seen. Then we readers came to another questionable passage.

> All: Our duty to your honor.
> Hamlet: Your loves, as mine to you. Farewell.

"Ooooo, they gay!" Mario announced, and the class was off laughing again.

"They are not gay!" I assured everybody over the riot that once again filled the room. "Really they aren't!"

"Sure they aren't," Mario said, sarcastically.

"No, really," I continued. "In Shakespeare's day, the word 'love' could be used interchangeably with the word 'like.' Hamlet is just calling upon their friendship to keep his secret."

"We believe you, Mrs. Webster," Percy said. "It's just that if Shakespeare meant 'friendship' why didn't he just say 'friendship' instead of 'love'?"

Now I was trapped—outsmarted by my own logic—with my own words.

"Percy, you and the class are going to have to trust me on this. When Shakespeare wrote this play almost 500 years ago, the language was English—even what we call Modern English, but it had many words we no longer use, and it has other words that are used differently now. Hamlet is asking his friends to keep his secret about the ghost, but these men are not gay! At least not in the sense you mean it."

"How do you know?" Avery asked, shocking everyone by his involvement in the discussion. "They might have been."

"Well, they might have been beekeepers, too," I answered,

"but there is no evidence to support that idea either. You have to go by what words are there, and what words are there are governed by the usage of the time."

"Well, I read somewhere that Shakespeare was gay," Tamara inserted, trying to milk this tangent dry and keep us off the subject of our lesson.

"Well, don't let his wife and children hear you," I said as I tried to get us back on track.

"But what if he was?" she asked insistently. "Having a wife and kids is no guarantee that he wasn't a homosexual."

"Tamara, what I think about Shakespeare's sex life is irrelevant to the study of this play, and it has never mattered to me what sexual orientation this writer had in his life. His words are still magnificent and moving and it doesn't matter. Now, would someone please take the part of Claudius and let's move on."

"Typical white teacher answer—hedging all around the truth," she said, apparently trying to bait me into further discussion.

I could feel more heat rising to my face. My anger was growing steadily hotter, so I took a deep breath. I was not going to be drawn into a racial battle with Tamara. Not today at least.

"Whatever," I said, calmly. "Now, let's get back to Hamlet and the 'ho's.'"

The class twittered slightly, Percy grinned at my little joke, and we all went on to finish most of the next scene before the bell rang to dismiss the class.

LESSON 21

The verb lie means "to rest" or "to recline," "to remain in a lying position." Its principal parts are lie, lying, lay, (have) lain. The verb lie never takes an object.

The verb lay means "to put" or "to place" (something). Its principal parts are lay, laying, laid, (have) laid. These forms may have objects (receivers of action).

Warriner's English Composition and Grammar
Third Level

I walked into the teachers' lounge on the third Friday of January as if I were a zombie. I had been doing extraordinarily well, I thought. I had kept up with the readings and lessons. I had finally gotten an overhead projector that worked, and I had discovered this clay-like substance that would keep my posters up on the walls and off the floor. I had even survived the rigors of the holidays. The only problem I had, however, was readjusting to the lack of sleep that non-holiday times seemed to create. I was always praying for the weekends when I could sleep until I wasn't tired any more. I also needed weekends so I could get ahead on my readings and caught up on my grading. Next year, I told myself often, I would do a better job of preparing myself during the summer months. I would find out just before summer vacation what classes I'd be teaching the next term so I could spend some of my down time getting myself organized and ready for the students.

As I shuffled into the noisy, cluttered teachers' lounge, I slowly moved to the Coke machine and inserted my money. With my caffeine-laden drink, I was hoping to get a boost of energy for the last few classes after lunch. I took a seat at an empty chair at the center table and groaned as I sat.

"You are much too young to be sounding so old," a familiar and friendly face said to me.

"Oh, Lydia, I am feeling rather old today for some reason," I said with a laugh.

"First year teacher, eh?" a male teacher at the table asked.

"Does it show that badly?"

"Only under your eyes," Lydia said. "Donna Webster, you do know Geoffrey Smythe from English Department, don't you?"

"Oh, yes. We get together all the time during department meetings."

Smythe was a middle-aged veteran teacher, a little paunchy and bald as an ostrich egg. He wore glasses, probably from years of close work and reading and he was very pale, especially in contrast to the dark green dress shirt that he wore.

"So, how's it going?" he asked.

"Not too badly," I said. "I'm just not used to getting so little sleep."

"You mean you never pulled 'all nighters' in college?" he asked, not even looking up from the stack of papers he was grading.

"No way," I assured him. "I have to have eight hours of sleep or I come apart at the seams. Why, I could just crawl up here on this table and just lay here for a while."

Smythe's head shot up and he looked me squarely in the face. "Lie!" he said emphatically.

"Excuse me?" I wasn't sure what I had lied about, but I was certain I hadn't said anything offensive, or so I thought.

"The word you are looking for, my dear colleague, is 'lie,'" he said, his nose in the air as if he's just smelled some objectionable thing. "You want to crawl up on this table and LIE down upon it."

"Of course," I said, horribly embarrassed when I realized my mistake. I blushed a deep red, for sure.

"It is a shame colleges can't do a better job of preparing teachers," he said in a half-mumbled insult.

"Lighten up, Geoffrey," Lydia said, realizing my discomfort. "It's a common enough error. Besides, Donna was just making pleasant conversation. She wasn't writing a term paper or an essay for your class."

"That is no excuse," he continued emphatically. "Teachers have to set an example. How can we possibly get these low-life students to speak properly if we don't do it ourselves?"

I was beginning to feel a good cry coming on as their conversation about me and my shortcomings continued. How could I have been so stupid? I thought. I could just kick myself. Now, I will forever be an intellectual slug to this stuffy little man, not that that should matter, but for some reason it did.

"But, Geoffrey, you just don't correct people in front of others. It's wrong to embarrass people in that way."

"Well, anyone who can't speak properly after four years of college deserves to be embarrassed."

Lydia was not going to let this lie. "Don't you know it's bad manners to try to make someone uncomfortable in public? I mean, manners were invented so we could get along in public situations with a minimum of discomfort. Correcting someone's grammar is just plain bad manners."

"Well, how else are people to learn what they have to know?" he asked.

"You don't have to humiliate anyone to teach them something," she said.

"Oh, but you do. Students need a little humbling to get them to avoid doing a given behavior again. And teachers most definitely need to know their subjects well enough to practice them in public."

"But that sounds like you're training dogs with avoidance therapy or something."

"Well, aren't we?" he asked.

"You know, Geoffrey," Lydia said, after a moment's thought, "what they say about you is true. You are an insufferable asshole."

I drew a sharp breath. I couldn't help myself.

"I don't have to take that kind of abuse," he snapped.

"Oh, yes, you do," Lydia said as anger grew more apparent in her voice. "I have hated people like you for years. I hate it when I go to a party where I know people like you are. I hate it because I have to be soooo careful. I never know when you're likely to swoop down on me and correct my ass in front of God and everybody. What makes you think you're such a paragon of virtue?"

"Well!" he said, collecting his papers and rising from his chair. As he left the room in a flurry of papers and pages, he slammed the door as he went.

Suddenly, the place erupted with applause. I jumped with startled surprise, since I really hadn't noticed the others in the room when all of this was going on.

"You tell him, Girl," one of the teachers said after she came over and patted Lydia on the back. "He's been getting on my nerves for years. Whoa! You were good! And Donna, honey, you don't have to listen to Mister Candy Pants anymore."

"That's right, Donna," Mr. Gleason, the football coach said. "Don't pay Mr. Smythe there any attention."

I smiled at all the friendly faces surrounding me.

"Are you okay, baby?" Lydia asked me.

"Yes," I said, laughing, "but I'm still tired enough to LAY down on this table."

Everyone laughed, and I stopped feeling bad. I even felt pretty good. Even though I may have made an enemy of Mr. Smythe and

I would need to avoid him in department meetings from now on, I knew I had a good number of new friends.

"Donna, you're all right by me," Lydia said. The bell rang signaling us to go to the next class.

LESSON 22

"Yes, ladies and gentlemen, the referee is signaling but the contender keeps raining the blows on Joe Louis. It's another to the body, and it looks like Louis is going down."

My race groaned. It was our people falling. It was another lynching, yet another Black man hanging in a tree. One more woman ambushed and raped. A Black boy whipped and maimed. It was hounds on the trail of a man running through slimy swamps. It was a white woman slapping her maid for being forgetful.

The men in the Store stood away from the walls and at attention. Women greedily clutched the babes on their laps while on the porch the shufflings and smiles and flirtings and pinching of a few minutes before were gone. This might be at the end of the world. If Joe lost we were back in slavery and beyond help. It would be true, the accusations that we were lower types of human beings.

I Know Why the Caged Bird Sings
Maya Angelou

Reginald may not have been the symbolic savior of his people the way Joe Louis had been in Maya Angelou's portrayal, but he could have made a giant step forward for the black youth in this community if only he had tried. He was that tall, lanky young man in my fifth-period class. He was good looking with his shaved head and mahogany dark skin, and he was as smart as any person I had ever met. That first quarter I knew Reginald, he proved to be my star pupil. He could read and understand anything I gave the class, and he did it with great ease. He wrote with a smoothness of style that would have made my picky college professors take notice.

On a less academic level, Reginald was a wonder at sports; not playing them but figuring the odds for them. He knew every basketball, baseball, hockey, football and track player there was in the world. He knew their stats, their achievements and their major plays in a variety of contests. He had amazing recall of games and plays, and all the kids turned to him when they wanted to know anything about upcoming games.

By the beginning of the second quarter, however, things really changed with Reginald. He stopped coming to class. It was weeks before I saw him again and by then he had failed since he hadn't done most assignments or taken most tests. Even though Reginald had an IQ close to 140 or 150 and he was a whiz at figuring the odds, he had turned that genius toward something else. He had discovered how many quality points he needed to pass each class. With his "A" from me for that first quarter and a "D" for the second, he knew he didn't need to do anything more for the rest of the year in order to pass. He could then skip all of his classes for the remaining two quarters and still pass on to the next grade.

There was really little any of us could do to get Reginald back into the classroom. The law threatened to take away his driver's license, but he didn't have a car to drive. The deans had threatened him with Saturday detentions, but if they couldn't get him there for the regular days, why would they think he'd come on Saturday as a punishment?

For some reason, he occasionally showed up on the Fridays that my class played a modified version of Trivial Pursuit. All students wanted him on their team because they were assured of victory. I was naturally flattered when he deigned to come to my class, and I vowed that somehow I'd convince him to come back to school so his considerable intellect could influence and hopefully inspire his less brilliant peers.

One Friday afternoon when he had come, before he could leave for the weekend, I was able to corner him before he could escape.

"Reginald, why don't you come back to school full-time and make a name for yourself? It's too late for you to be a National Merit Scholar, but I'm sure you could get a different scholarship if you'd just take the SAT. Then, I'd put money on it that you could go to any school in the country. It's just that you need to come back to class and finish."

"Mrs. Webster, all I want to do in this life is work in my father's architectural firm. I'm already keeping his books, and he needs me. We're going to be partners as soon as I reach eighteen. I just don't need school."

I figured he was doing more than just working in an architectural firm. I didn't let on. From all accurate reports from the guidance counselors, Reginald was already eighteen and he didn't have a father or stepfather around. If he were keeping the books for anybody, it was probably a bookie or, worse yet, a drug dealer. Still, I played along with his little lie.

"Well, I'm glad you have plans, Reginald," I said with a smile, "but it never hurts to have a number of options open to you. Education is always a good investment in the future."

"Not for me," he said with such tremendous assurance that it startled me. "Maybe if I had 'invested' my time in some private school where I could get the background I need for higher math and more complicated writing, then I might be able to stand school."

"Do you really believe that you can't get in public school what you can in a private school?"

"Of course."

I looked at him with unbelieving, hurt eyes. He began to fidget.

"Look, Mrs. Webster, this school is a waste of my time. All we do is read novels and plays and poems and useless stuff like that. Dates and places. Just junk. Stuff I can't use in the real world."

"Reginald, I can't believe what I'm hearing," I said. "Surely, you can see the value of being able to write well and to comprehend accurately what you read. And what's wrong with novels and plays? They make movies and television shows and all sorts of pleasant things from them. Maybe you could even be someone who could produce some of those things. You must see that."

"Nope. Not really. Sorry, Mrs. Webster. I know you mean well, but all I want is enough money to enjoy the good life, and I can have that if I work for my dad. Besides I don't have anyone I can talk to here, except maybe you. I feel really out of place. Working with my dad has kept me from going nuts."

Reginald probably was out of place and going nuts. He was light years ahead of his classmates since he was always put in the lower level classes because of his poor report cards. He never tried to get into the honors level classes, probably because there he'd have to work a lot harder, and certainly longer than one or two quarters. Also, there he might not outshine anybody.

"Look, I have to catch my bus," he said nervously.

There was nothing left for me to say, except, "Okay, see you later."

He rushed out of my door and out of the school building forever, and I could feel a real defeat coming on. I wondered if I had tried hard enough. Maybe if I'd detained him a while longer I could have convinced him to come back. But my guess was that I'd be wasting my breath. For the first time I realized that I couldn't get through to everybody, and that was one of the hardest lessons for me to learn.

LESSON 23

Water, water everywhere,
And all the boards did shrink.
Water, water, everywhere,
Nor any drop to drink.

The Rime of the Ancient Mariner
Samuel Coleridge

The sorrowful thing about Thomas was everybody liked him. Everybody would have given him the shirt off his or her back if he'd have taken it. Everyone wanted to see him succeed; but no matter what we did to help him, he shunned our efforts and headed off on a self-destructive course that none but he could change.

At the beginning of the year when I first met Thomas, he was one of the cutest and wittiest children in the room. He was very slight—less than five feet tall, if he was that tall—and here he was in his senior year. At the beginning he was stylishly dressed, but as the days passed, his expensive dress clothes were slowly being replaced by a more casual and hip attire—tee shirts and low-slung, baggy jeans. Soon his actions began to match his attire. His grades began to slip, then his attendance.

After a long spell of not seeing him, I asked the Dean of Boys, Mr. Allison, where Thomas might be. He told me Thomas was in jail for car theft, and it would be quite some time before he'd be back in my class again. Maybe I could send some assignments so he could keep up.

I was shocked and horrified all at the same time. Thomas had been so likeable. It was unimaginable to me he could have done anything criminal. He was so cute. Surely there had been a mistake. Surely it was a case of mistaken identity or something like that.

His even littler and cuter brother, Jonathan, came to see me on a regular basis to let me know how Thomas was doing. I would pass along greetings and encouragement, and I'd get the latest news on how the trial was progressing. The guidance counselors and I even wrote letters to the district attorney saying we had known or taught Thomas for a long, collective period of time and he was a model student; he was truly quite nice and a fine young man.

"He's coming home this week, Ms. Webster," Jonathan told me sometime around the end of January. "That means he should be back in class around Monday."

"What happened at the trial?"

"He was convicted."

"And his sentence?"

"Time-served, two years probation, $500 fine, 200 hours community service, and he has to be in class every day until the end of the school year."

"I'm surprised his punishment is so stiff. I thought they adjudicated things differently for a first offense."

"It wasn't his first offense," Jonathan said.

"Oh," I said, turning my eyes away so he wouldn't see the surprise on my face or the disappointment in my eyes.

That Monday came and so did Thomas, who sat as big, or

little, as you please in his usual desk like nothing had ever happened or was any different. His behavior was, however, unusually subdued for Thomas. He did not offer any of his funny quips or playful banter as he used to do. Now he was almost sullen, but if provoked he would quickly fly into an uncharacteristic rage.

"What you taking my paper for, fool!" he bellowed at his neighbor who had taken a sheet of notebook paper from his neat little stack of papers on his desk.

"Sorry, man," the other boy said, quickly returning the piece of paper. "I just thought I could have some since we used to share all the time."

"Well, you thought wrong!" Thomas said angrily, snatching the paper from his hand and then crumpling it up.

As the weeks passed, he became more and more uncooperative, just doing the least amount of work he could get away with and not participating in any discussion as he would have done before his arrest. Occasionally he demonstrated the spark of that wit that often had me doubled over along with the rest of the class.

"What the hell is this sailor man doing shooting at birds for anyway?" he asked when we were reading *The Rime of the Ancient Mariner*. "Man, I don't get how a stupid bird or whatever it was, could give a man such bad luck."

"The bird itself didn't give him bad luck . . ."

"Looks like pretty bad luck to me when all your crew is dying of the thirst and floating around all ghost-like. Pretty damn bad luck, I'd say."

I had to laugh as did others in the room. His animated gestures and squeaky voice were pretty funny.

I continued to try to clarify the story for him by saying, "KILLING the albatross caused the bad luck, Thomas, not the albatross itself. Killing the bird was a wasteful, wanton act, sort of like companies that squander natural resources—like strip mining companies which strip all the land of its life just to get at a few minerals beneath it."

Or like young men who steal automobiles that don't belong to them and ruin their chances at having a good life in the process, I thought inside my head.

"Whatever," Thomas replied. Then he put his head on his desk and didn't offer another sound for the rest of the class.

He was still amusing when it came to artwork. One assignment I had given this particular quarter was for students to design and construct masks representing characters from any of the stories or plays we had read. Thomas' mask didn't conform to the assignment at all. It was merely a clever caricature of himself, complete with imagined beard and pea patch hairdo. A paper-clip earring dangled from one of the ears. Even though he hadn't followed the assignment's directions at all, there was no mistaking who had made his mask.

Toward the end of the term Thomas brought a camera to class and took some pictures of students. Since we were on schedule with our work load, I let him take a few extra candids and even posed myself with some of the girls he had grouped together.

Then, class proceeded and ended without incident. The final bell for the day rang and the students all poured out of my room, out of the building and into the afternoon. I went to my desk to organize my papers for that night's grading session. As I worked quietly, Lydia came in my door and asked if I had, by any slim chance, seen her camera. It had been taken from a drawer in her desk several periods before while she was on break.

My heart dropped. "What did it look like?"

"Well, it was a Nikon 35mm with zoom lens and strobe flash and . . ."

"Thomas had a camera just like that today," I said.

"Thomas Johnson? The little funny guy in the Senior Class who's been in jail already for stealing cars?"

"That's the one."

"Damn," she said softly, "I bet it's already sold, and I won't ever see it again." She then hurriedly left the room to report her suspicions to the dean.

"Damn," I said softly to myself as I realized then Thomas

probably had not learned much from his time spent in jail. He hadn't learned his lesson about stealing, and he hadn't learned that he truly was the master of his own fate—that only he could make his life work. We would all mourn as he plotted such a dangerous course through very troubled waters no matter how hard we tried to dissuade him.

FEBRUARY

LESSON 24

These are the times that try men's souls. The summer soldier
and the sunshine patriot will in this crisis, shrink from the
service of his country; but he that stands it NOW, deserves
the love and thanks of man and woman.

"The American Crisis"
Thomas Paine

I kept playing Thomas Paine's words over and over in my
head the infamous day I cried—yes, cried in front of the
class—when I was so exasperated that I could find no other outlet
than hot, stinging tears. I also remembered poor old Madame
Finkelstein, my high school French teacher, who cried at least once
a week. For the first time in my life I felt sorry for her and
understood her sorrow. I knew at last the humiliation and horror
which can be meted out by one's students.

Of course, I quickly removed myself from the room before any
tears actually spilled, but the students knew. Some saw me later in
the day, my eyes puffy and red. And my neck does this horrible
thing where it gets all these red blotches on it when I become

emotional. I was a mess. These signs absolutely delighted one of my students. Tamara, as a matter of fact.

Paine's passage didn't happen to be the lesson for the day for my seniors when all hell broke loose. I had been teaching his work in my junior classes, and that is why it came to mind when my time with Tamara began to "try my soul."

In my senior classes we were reading the part in *Gulliver's Travels* when Gulliver is in Lilliput. Tamara exhaled loudly and said, "How come we got to read this stupid white man's trash anyhow?"

"Tamara, why do I have to go over this with you again? Haven't we hashed this out enough?"

Her face held a defiant, hateful smirk that dared me to explain myself.

"Okay. Once again, you need to read this 'white man's trash,' as you put it, if you want to be able to compete with other American students who are going to college. You need to know what Jonathan Swift said and you need to know about the travels of his character Gulliver."

"The same old crap," she said as she turned in her desk and addressed the other students.

"What does that mean?" I should never have asked.

"What that means is you, a white woman, think you can come in here with your Christian ways and take care of us pick-a-ninny, 'nigga chi'rn' and then go back to your comfortable white world while the rest of us rot here in the ghetto."

My mouth must have fallen open and my eyes must have begun to brim with tears, I wasn't sure. All I could do was try to understand her words now reeling in my brain. What evil had I ever done this child? Why was her hatred so pointed toward me?

Percy came immediately to my defense. "Tamara, you need to hold on yourself. You are so out of line."

Mario said, "Yeah, give the woman a break. She's just doing her job."

"Yeah," many others agreed.

"And another thing," Tamara continued as if the resistance

from her peers was making her stronger. "Your hair makes you look like some kind of palomino or something, and you look pregnant in those ugly clothes you wear!"

Her attack was so bizarre I could hardly fathom its cause. She was also loud, so loud I was unaware that there were vehement protests on the part of the other students. I took a deep breath to keep the tears at bay and tried to continue with the lesson.

"All that aside," I said shakily, "I still have to teach this man's work. When I get to Frederick Douglass, I will wake you up."

"What you mean by saying that, you raggedy-assed bitch!"

A choking silence fell. Calmly, I went to my desk, got the discipline referral out of the center drawer of my desk and wrote upon it.

> Tamara is causing sufficient disruption that I cannot teach my lesson. She is also calling me names such as "raggedy-assed bitch," which I do not appreciate.
>
> D. Webster

I handed the referral to Tamara and told her to report to the dean of girls immediately. She took the referral with a vicious snatch and began to read it.

"Disruption?" she yelled. "I'll show you disruption!"

She rushed up to my desk and with a sweeping gesture of her arm, she knocked everything to the floor. My books and papers were reduced to a mangled pile of rubble and my new potted cactus plant shattered when it hit the ground. Dirt was strewn everywhere, and the girl stood in the center of it shaking with rage, all the fury made manifest, as she would have me believe, from centuries of slavery and racial discrimination. I suspected it came from years of deliberate training—the kind that paints all whites as "blue-eyed devils." And I don't even have blue eyes, I thought.

It was a horrible stand-off. Percy had risen from his seat and was moving toward the front. The rest of the class waited to see what I would do. I trembled violently inside, but I was able to conceal it from the class. It was all I could do to walk calmly to the panic button on the wall and muster up enough strength to push it.

"Do you have an emergency?" the tinny voice from the wall asked.

"I need a student removed from my room immediately."

"On our way."

Tamara backed up to her desk as if someone might jump her. I stayed at the wall, hoping she would not touch me. Thankfully, I could see Percy's entire 6'3" presence as he calmly stepped between her and me just in case she were to go ballistic again.

Both deans arrived and surveyed the damage and then prepared to escort the arrogant, hostile Tamara to her punishment.

"Where's the referral?" Mr. Allison asked.

"I gave it to her," I said. "I'm not sure what she did with it."

"Tamara, where's the referral?"

"She lies! She didn't give me nothin'!" Tamara almost spat the words in my direction.

Before I could even respond, the room broke into a major condemnation of Tamara and a barrage of accusations rose from the ranks. Many students came to my defense, but my trembling only increased, and I felt my knees begin to buckle.

Someone located the crumpled up document in Tamara's desk and gave it to the dean of girls. Ms. Weller read it, looked at Tamara, and shook her head. Then, taking either arm of the child, the discipline entourage made its way out of my classroom and out of sight.

After a few moments with all eyes upon me, I walked to my desk, surveyed the damage and broke into tears.

"Excuse me," I choked as I made my way out into the hall where I sobbed openly.

Soon there was a tap on the closed door from the inside and a soft, feminine voice asked, "May I come out and talk to you?"

"Not yet," I sobbed, but the door opened anyway and Marvelette stepped through.

Marvelette was a delightful young woman whose mother named her for her favorite singing group of the same name. She had described herself as a strawberry blonde, although I didn't see it so. Her dark hair did indeed have a red hue, but there was no blonde about it. Her hair was black hair that had been colored. Still, I didn't argue.

Her skin was relatively light, the color of cafe au lait and equally creamy. And she was round, no sharp edges, just soft full curves. I had liked Marvelette a great deal before, but today I would come to love her.

With a kindness I had rarely known, she put her warm arms around me and hugged me tenderly. This made the tears really pour, and I lost all emotional control. She just kept holding me as she patted my back as if I were just a little baby.

"It's all right, Ms. Webster," she kept saying over and over again. "We all love you."

I kept crying and Marvelette held me gently until the bell rang, and it was time for my planning period.

Tamara would not return for ten days—five days suspension being the price one pays for cursing a teacher at this school and an additional five for the wanton destruction of my personal property. My task was to call her parents and see whether we could somehow alter her behavior.

True to form, when I finally got through on the always-busy phone line, Tamara got on the phone herself and pretended to be her mother. Not believing any kid capable of such a deception, I talked at length with the person I thought was the mother. In monosyllabic words, the voice agreed that her "daughter's" behavior would improve, and it did for the first week she was back. Then, Tamara began slipping into sleep at the beginning of each class, and only the final bell would wake her from her slumbers. I felt a twinge of guilt about not waking her until I overheard her say to a student she'd make me cry again if she didn't pass this particular quarter. She didn't pass, and this time her parents came out in full show of support for their poor "wronged Tamara."

"You teachers need to communicate with us parents so we can assist in correcting student misbehavior," the Reverend Brown, her stern-faced father, said forcefully to me. He was the minister of the local evangelical church just around the corner and quite a pillar of the black community.

"But I spoke with your wife on the phone not four weeks ago. She assured me Tamara's behavior would improve," I defended myself.

"You never spoke with me," Mrs. Brown said.

"I spoke with someone at this number who said she was you." I showed her my phone log sheet with the date, time, and name of the person with whom I thought I had spoken.

"Tamara?" the reverend said, looking over at his daughter.

"I don't know anything about that," she said with her usual contemptuous air.

The good reverend's hand came up to strike her, and immediately Tamara began to confess her deceit.

"All right, I pretended to be Mama, but Ms. Webster was so stupid, like she couldn't tell it was me. What a fool!"

The hand came down hard across her face with a hideous smacking sound. My eyes grew as wide as they could get, and Tamara's eyes turned toward me and smoldered with hate. Without any tears, they glared at me.

"I don't ever want to hear you say such things about or to your teachers, even if they are white. Do you hear me?" he asked.

"Yes, sir," she said, trembling with rage.

"This is the last time you'll shame me in front of a white person," he said venomously. He then took a deep breath, looked my way and said, "No offense."

I began to understand Tamara a lot better after that conference. She never ever came to like me or my class, and she never passed it either. She would have to pass English with a summer school teacher, one who would know better how to deal with her. At least for the rest of my time with her, she sat stoically in her desk, arms folded and eyes staring hatefully at me as I did my job. Thankfully, she never confronted me again, and for that I was terribly grateful.

LESSON 25

Water. W,a,t,e,r. Water. It has a—name—(and now the miracle happens. Helen drops the pitcher on the slant under the spout, it shatters. She stands transfixed. Annie freezes on the pump handle; there is a change in the sundown light, and with it a change in Helen's face, some light we have never seen there, some struggle in the depths behind it; and her lips tremble, trying to remember something the muscles around them once knew, till at last it found its way out, painfully a baby sound buried under some debris of years of dumbness.)

Helen: Wah. Wah.

(And again with great effort)

Wah. Wah.

(Helen plunges her hand into the dwindling water, spells into her own palm. Then she gropes frantically, Annie reaches for her hand, and Helen spells into Annie's hand.)

Annie:(whispering). Yes.

(Helen spells it out again.) Yes!

The Miracle Worker
William Gibson

One wonderfully lazy February Sunday, the kind when Michael and I didn't emerge from bed until 11:00 or 11:30, we were taking it easy. It was one of those gray, freezing Florida winter days that sent us natives inside whining about the cold. Since we decided not to go to church, had no other place to go, and we certainly didn't want to go outside, we opted for a leisurely brunch where we could sip coffee and read the thick newspaper until we were tired of it.

I had read through all the world news headlines and articles that I wanted and was on my way into the "Metro," or local, section of the paper when my eyes fell upon a headline that stopped me cold.

"Schools Fail Again," it said, and almost before I could take another sip of coffee, I was deep into a local politician's tirade about what he thought was wrong with the schools. This man, a member of the Urban League, felt that inner city schools were not providing the quality education that was being given to suburban schools or those with a preponderance of white children. He blamed the teachers for the lack of student performance, because "any good educator can teach any children whatever it is they need to know."

As my eyes skimmed over his hateful words, I could feel my stomach tighten and my jaw tense. My color became a hot-red and I ceased being in a good mood. Once again, I felt that I was being held responsible for the care and well being of an entire society after having been given negligible support.

"Nothing in the world makes me madder than someone criticizing something they don't understand," I announced to Michael. "How can this guy say these things? I've never once seen him at my school, and I certainly haven't seen him in my classroom."

"What are you talking about?" Michael asked as he looked up from his section of the paper.

"You've got to read this garbage," I said, indicating the place where he should begin.

As he read the piece, I grumbled and mumbled all sorts of

angry thoughts to myself. "Where are you guys when funding time rolls around and we have to cut teachers and our class loads go over 40 per room? Where are you when some child gets it into her head to trash my room because I have the audacity to teach the state's curriculum? Where are you when I'm trying to read my third different chapter in the texts so that I can be conversant with the children the next day?"

"Write a letter," Michael said quietly.

"What?"

"I said for you to write a letter—one to the editor of the newspaper."

"Really?"

"How are they going to know that this guy is an ignorant jerk if you don't say something and let them know?"

"But it seems that people who write letters to the editor are often crackpots, if you know what I mean."

"Maybe," Michael said as he spread jelly on his last piece of toast, "it's just that these guys can say whatever they like and people will believe them, if the rest of us don't take them to task."

"You may have a point."

I mulled it over all Sunday, and finally, after I had finished my three hours of homework, I sat at my computer and carefully composed my letter.

Editor of *The Florida Times Union*
123 Riverside Avenue
Jacksonville, FL 32207

Dear Sir:

Anne Sullivan was a teacher, "a miracle worker." She took a young girl who was deaf, blind, and mute and opened the world to her. This real life story was a great inspiration to me as a young woman. I am sure it was instrumental in my becoming a teacher. I had hoped that on a less dramatic scale, I could open the eyes, ears, and mouths of young people so that they could communicate in their vast and difficult world.

This year, however, I am as discouraged as Anne Sullivan ever could be. I am told by a member of the Urban League in an article that ran in your paper last Sunday that I don't have "the right formula" to prepare the children for the future. I am told Johnny and Jane can't read, write or think, because I am not doing what needs to be done. I am part of a system that holds back too many non-functioning children, which destroys their egos, but then we'd better not graduate anyone who is ill-prepared to be a productive citizen or a competent worker. Include also a considerable disrespect that is seeping into the attitudes of children and their parents. Add to that discipline problems which prevent me from teaching any lessons, much less important ones, and I'll give you a formula for despair.

My teaching load has just this month been tapered down to 148. That is a 1:29 ratio and not the 1:20 ratio the state would have the public believe. I had to take on a third preparation because my school lost four English positions at appropriation time, so I am working out of three literature books and three grammar books. I have three different sets of novels to teach and three sets of plays. I have been threatened with physical violence and cursed and mocked by the children I seek to serve, and there are days when I am about ready to throw in the towel.

I am a good teacher! I could be another Anne Sullivan, a "miracle worker;" but Anne Sullivan had only one student. She was able to be with her student 24 hours a day and she was able to remove her student from the outside influences of her life. Who couldn't work miracles under those circumstances?

I don't know why I feel so defensive when I read the *Times Union*'s report on the analysis of the State's report card, but I will assure any citizen in this county I am teaching as hard as I can.

Sincerely,
Donna K. Webster
Language Arts Teacher
Paul Lawrence Dunbar Senior High School

I never sent the letter to the newspaper because just writing it made me feel a little better about my job. I guess the Tamara incident had really made me wonder if teaching was a job I could do for the rest of my career life. Then, with the story in the newspaper shouting at me how unappreciated my efforts are, well, I was understandably distressed. I reasoned that most of education's critics haven't stepped into the classroom since they were kids. They don't have the faintest clue as to how difficult it is to teach anymore. Actually, it has never been easy to teach. It's just that now I am in the thick of it. I can see what a demanding job it is and how little credit for our successes we educators are given. Everybody's a critic, and we can't do the job of educating the youth of a nation without considerable help from everybody.

No, I never sent the letter, but it made me feel better just writing what was on my mind. Maybe the next time I read another scathing article, I'll dust off this letter and put it in the mail.

LESSON 26

The telescreen received and transmitted simultaneously. Any sound that Winston made, above the level of a very low whisper, would be picked up by it; moreover, so long as he remained within the field of vision which the metal plaque commanded, he could be seen as well as heard. There was of course no way of knowing whether you were being watched at any given moment. How often, or on what system, the Thought Police plugged in on any individual wire was guesswork. It was even conceivable that they watched everybody all the time.

But at any rate they could plug in your wire whenever they wanted to. You had to live—did live, from habit that became instinct—in the assumption that every sound you made was overheard, and, except in darkness, every movement scrutinized.

1984
George Orwell

I t was the kind of cold day that makes most humans long for the tranquil, gentle days of spring and summer. The sky was a steel gray and ominous, and rain, maybe even snow, was sure to arrive before the day was out. I was still cold even after putting on my heaviest Florida clothes and coat, and I cursed myself inwardly for having allowed myself to become so accustomed to the mostly balmy climate of my home. I have always hated February and its cold fronts.

My hands were brittle as they tried to maneuver the icy-cold steering wheel. My spirits were as downcast and solemn as the pitiful hum from my not-so-hot heater. I wasn't really in the mood to teach today. I'd much rather be snuggled up in my bed covers than in front of a rather-be-in-bed-too class. When would the summer ever come? I thought as I drove my frigid way to school.

When I arrived at Dunbar, the weather had not improved. The sky seemed even darker, and a fine mist was now coating my windshield. This made the school building an uncharacteristically inviting place. I couldn't wait to get into its warmth. I gingerly made the trek from my car to the building and rushed into the warm, enveloping air of the lobby.

As I stepped in, I immediately bumped into a uniformed figure who turned out to be a local policeman.

"I'm so sorry," I said. "Hey, Officer Arnold, what're you doing here?"

"Another break-in and more TV's are gone."

"Not again," I said, shaking my head in disbelief.

"Yep, and this time they did a lot of other damage."

The principal came over to us, actually to the officer, and started a conversation of which I obviously was not to be a part.

"Excuse me," I said awkwardly and moved on to my classroom.

As I made my way down the halls, the devastation of the crime spree was readily visible. Crowbar marks appeared at the lock of every door on the hall I traveled. Broken glass from some of the transom windows littered the floor. Only a small portion had been swept into piles janitors feverishly tried to remove before the onslaught of the students. Dread filled me as I neared my room. Of course, it had not been spared. My door stood ajar and violated. As I carefully stepped into my room, cold wind whistled through the broken window where someone had apparently tried to make either an entry or an escape.

When I flipped on the light a horrible sight filled my eyes. The thief or thieves had knocked over my book cases and up-ended most of my plants, cracking their pots and for the third time this year, my cactus garden lay violated on the floor. My fichus tree lay on its side, its giant pot cracked open, and my TV was gone—pulled from its perch on the wall and leaving an ugly, unpainted bare spot where it had been. My room looked like a bomb had gone off in it, and I just wanted to lose my composure right there. There wasn't time, though. The bell would ring in a few minutes, and I had to get as much of this mess cleaned up as quickly as possible.

As I bent down to pick up the first book, the PA crackled on and said, "To all teachers whose rooms have been vandalized. Do NOT—I repeat—do NOT touch anything in your room. The police are sending investigators to dust for prints and to make other assessments. Direct all your students to the auditorium when the bell rings. Please stay with your students until further notice."

I got to spend the first half of the day in the auditorium with my first period class, and I hesitate to call it a class. It really was more like a free-for-all. Since there were twenty other classes of students in there and another twenty or so in the gym, teaching for the entire school was suspended for the day. All I had to do was to keep my little section of the auditorium from going berserk, and that was about all I could handle. They should have canceled school for the day, I thought, but that would require we make this day up during the summer, and NO one wanted that.

While I graded the papers I had left untouched in my briefcase from the night before, the students in my class played all sorts of chanting games and paper games and eventually started a paper-wad basketball game. By noon I was very tired of sitting and trying to concentrate over the noise, and by noon the kids were beyond antsy. Thankfully, lunch was served in the cafeteria at its usual time, and then we were instructed to go back to our usual classrooms for our sixth-period to finish out the day.

By the time we were allowed back into the building, the police had left. My room felt like a meat locker, but then I had been uncomfortably cold all day. The window would take a few days to repair, and I would simply have to make the appropriate adjustments. So all bundled up in our coats and jackets, my sixth period students and I began to fix up my room as best we could. The guys righted the bookcase and propped the fichus tree up in a corner on newspaper until I could replace its pot. Some of the girls put all the books back for me. Another of my students carefully swept up the shards of pottery, while I carefully placed the damaged plants on wet paper toweling until I could find new homes for them. I was getting pretty good at this plant restoration business.

As we worked, there was a lot of idle talk about the incident.

"What makes people be so mean, Mrs. Webster?" Arthina asked.

"Search me," I answered with extreme profoundness.

"I bet someone is making a whole shit pot full of money stealing this stuff," Mario said. "Oh, sorry, Mrs. Webster."

"I hear you," I answered.

"Yeah, but who would want to buy school board stuff? Ain't nobody I know'd want those clunker TV's," Roscoe said.

"But pawn shops'll buy 'em," Thomas offered. None of us was surprised that Thomas had such knowledge.

"But pawn shops can't do that," I said. "They could get into real, MAJOR trouble buying stolen goods."

"You really believe that, don't you, Mrs. Webster?" Thomas asked.

"I guess I figure since I follow the rules, so does everyone else. I guess I'm pretty naive, huh?"

"Yes, Ma'am. You sure are," Thomas assured me, and everyone around me nodded.

"I heard some policemen talking in the lunchroom," Arthina said. "They were saying we are going to put up surveillance cameras in the halls and bathrooms."

"What?" I asked. "Who told you this?"

"I said I heard Officer Arnold say it to one of the other policemen. I don't think they knew I was listening."

"I think you must be mistaken, Arthina," I said. "I really don't think there is the money for that, especially now that we have lost so much equipment. Besides, I think some sort of civil rights are violated when you put cameras in the bathrooms."

"Yeah," Shamika said, "I won't even shop in a store where they say they watch you through the mirrors."

"What makes you think all stores don't watch you anywhere already?" Roscoe asked. "Just 'cause some say they are watching you doesn't mean the others don't. They just don't tell you."

"Go on!" Shamika gasped at the very idea.

"What are you talking about, fool?" Mario asked.

"I'm saying we are watched all the time, just like old Winston Smith in that book we read."

"Roscoe, I am so pleased you have seen a connection between this situation and what was going on in *1984*," I said. "That means reading that book was not a waste of time."

"Humph," I thought I heard Thomas say.

"I think they are watching us even now," Roscoe continued.

"How?" I asked.

"Well, maybe they aren't watching as much as they are listening in over the intercom."

"I think we'd know if they were listening. The intercom does make a crackling noise when it comes on."

"Yeah, but what if it is left on all the time? You'd get used to that sound, wouldn't you?"

"You're just . . . what's the word, Ms. Webster?" Mario asked. "Paranoid?"

"Yeah, that's it. Paranoid."

"Maybe," Roscoe said, "but I still think it's possible."

I had never really thought about it before, but Roscoe had a point. How would we ever know? How could we tell if the intercom were left on all the time?

When the final bell rang that day, it was none too soon. The students ran from the building, and the faculty was about to do the same when the intercom crackled on.

"All teachers report to the library for an emergency faculty meeting."

I rolled my eyes, packed up my briefcase, turned off the lights, and left. When I went to lock my door, as was my habit, I remembered the lock was now broken and totally useless.

"I don't think I can go through another day like this any time soon," Elizabeth, one of my language arts colleagues, said to me as she came up behind me.

"Me either," I said as we walked the hall together to the library.

"What a shame we have to go through this so often!" she said.

"What a shame these kids have to go through this," I said.

"Humph."

After all the teachers were assembled, the principal announced that the recent rash of thefts had called for rash measures. The county had made arrangements for a security system within the week, but as an added deterrent, they were also going to put up surveillance cameras in the halls and in the restrooms.

There was a murmur that moved through the crowd. I realized then that the student information network was obviously a lot better than the teacher one.

"Isn't it a little late for us to worry with a security system? Most of the school's TV's are already stolen," a masculine voice in the back asked.

A nervous tremor of commentary moved through the faculty.

"We still have plenty of equipment we want to keep," the principal said.

"What do you think the cameras will do?" a female voice asked.

Our police officer stood up and said, "You can monitor activities not only of thieves, but of the children as well. It will be a real deterrent to bad behavior."

"But why the bathrooms?" another voice asked.

"Because it is so hard to man all the areas of the school, this should help us in our supervision of the children entrusted to our care," the principal said.

"But what about the children's civil rights?" a social studies teacher asked.

"Well, what about them? What about the children's civil right to have a safe school environment?" Mr. Ward, the principal, fired back in an angry voice that revealed his frustration and fatigue.

The discussion came to an abrupt halt, and the meeting became an informational session wherein announcements about other policies were made. Our input was obviously not desired.

After the meeting as I made my miserable way through the gloomy cold to my car, I began to feel a little bit like Winston Smith myself. I hated Februaries.

LESSON 27

A Man Among the Dead: My boy Joel was a sailor. Knew 'em all. He'd set on the porch evenings and tell 'em all by name. Yessir; wonderful . . .

And my boy Joel who knew the stars—he used to say it took millions of years for that speck of light to git to earth. Don't seem like a body could believe it, but that's what he used to say—millions of years.

Our Town
Thornton Wilder

Sometimes I wish I could read something again for the first time. I want to relive the wonder and joy I felt when I first read the words that moved me to tears or buoyed my spirits with inspiration. *Romeo and Juliet* was one of those literary events for me. So was *The Scarlet Letter*. But *Our Town* has held a very special place in my heart. It is special not only for what Emily discovers about life and has translated to me in the audience, but also because my husband played a part, actually two parts, in a local little theater production of the play. My husband, Michael, a big, burly football-coach-type, has a master's in English literature.

Of course we were college sweethearts, both of us English majors. We met, however, not in class, but on a blind date. My roommate had set us up with the help of her boyfriend, a fraternity brother of my future husband.

Michael and I passed my sophomore and junior year at Florida State University deeply in love, and we got married just before my senior year began. I finished my course work my senior year while we lived in married-student housing. It was a great adventure until he got a teaching job in Jacksonville, and I had to do my internship in Sopchoppy, Florida, alone. Those agonizing months of separation served only to remind me I did not want to live without him ever again. Now we both lived and taught English in the same county. He was assigned to Wolfson Senior High about fifteen miles from where I was assigned. And each night, after a brief nap and snuggle session, we often sat up reading lessons and grading papers and sharing stories about our adventures of the day. Of course, we never seemed to be doing the same material at the same time. While I was teaching juniors and seniors, he was teaching sophomores. I really didn't envy him. Sophomores can be extremely unruly, but Michael had to prepare only one set of lessons. I had considerably more to prepare. Oh, well, such was the luck of the first-year teacher as compared to the luck of a second-year teacher.

During the fall, a mutual friend had called and quite literally begged Michael to play the parts of Belligerent Man in the Audience and A Man Among the Dead in the Jacksonville Little Theater's spring production of *Our Town*. Michael was reluctant, fearing he wouldn't have the time, but I think he was basically worried about his raging stage fright, which could make his voice crack like that of a thirteen-year-old.

Michael finally agreed to help out and devoted several evenings a week to the preparation of the play—sometimes building props and other times working in rehearsals. When it was at last the day of the performance, he looked terrible because he hadn't gotten any sleep the night before. He tossed and turned and kept me awake as well. He could hardly eat a thing that next morning. He was afraid he'd lose his breakfast. I did what I could to encourage and support him, but there is little anyone can do for the actor when he is facing his own private fear.

Leanne, bless her, had taken me seriously when I offered extra credit to any student going to a theatrical performance. She had remembered what I had said in passing about my husband being in a play, and she told me after class one day that she really wanted to come to see the performance. Would I please meet her at the front of the Little Theater on opening night so we could sit together to watch? Of course I would.

I was thrilled that she was interested. I still couldn't get over how much alike Leanne and I were. She loved the same books that I loved. We both liked the same movies, and we both shared a fondness for live theater.

Unlike me, Leanne could act. She had already been in a church presentation of *A Raisin in the Sun* and had gotten rave reviews from the neighborhood newspaper's theater critic. "Believable and sincere" were the words used to describe Leanne's performance, and when I attended the performance, I was mesmerized by her presence. It was too bad our school could not offer drama since none of the teachers were certified to teach it. We also had such an eagle-eyed bookkeeper who could find the least flaw in any accounting. Very few of us would take on clubs for fear we'd have to balance budgets with him.

"Leanne," I called, when I saw her dark brown head over that of the predominantly white-haired crowd of theater-goers. "Over here!"

She rushed over all aglow. "Aren't you excited?" she said as she came up beside me.

"You'd think I was performing tonight, I'm so nervous," I said. "Come on, let's get seated. I don't want to miss anything."

As we came down the aisle of the dark, old auditorium, I could just make out Michael in the center section.

"That's my husband," I said as I pointed in his direction. "He's playing the Belligerent Man and he performs his part from the audience, remember?"

"Really?"

"Yes, don't you remember about how he confronts the stage manager and all that?"

"Sort of."

We took our seats far from Michael so we wouldn't get in his way or upset his concentration. While we waited, I filled the time with idle conversation.

"How are things going for you?" I asked lamely.

"Fine," she answered.

"I mean, how are things going with your boyfriends." I wasn't very cool about this sort of thing.

She smiled when she realized that I was making reference to her little problem of a few months ago. "I've sorta put those sorts of thing on the back burner, if you know what I mean."

I breathed a deep sigh of relief that this conversation didn't need to continue any further in this difficult direction. I also was pleased to hear that she had, at least for the moment, heeded my advice. "And college? Have you started making plans?"

"Well, I'm looking into all the state schools, of course. Mom and I think we can afford those with a little help from loans and stuff. But I think I'd really rather go to a cool school—Smith maybe or Harvard. They are beyond our means, but if I do well enough on the SAT and get scholarships, I might be able to make it."

"Well, just let me know what I can do to help. Have you given any thought to a major yet?"

"Actually, I have. I'd love to go into teaching. English. I would probably want to teach at the college level, especially if I put all that time and effort into an Ivy League-type school, but I wouldn't mind teaching high school."

"You know, if I knew then what I know now, I sometimes wonder if I'd do this again," I heard myself say. "Teaching has been the hardest thing I have ever done in my life; but to be honest,

I would imagine the first year of any career has to be the hardest. I probably should give it a couple of years before I come in with a verdict on teaching."

"You make it look so fun," Leanne said.

I laughed at the very idea of fun. "If you could only see how hard I have to work to get it to look fun. I must put in one extra hour a night per class just to keep up and even then, I can get behind so easily."

"Still, you really make the subject come to life for me. And I can tell that the other kids feel the same way too. They are really crazy about you, you know."

"Me?" I was struck with a wave of joy at her words. I felt horribly flushed. Then, the thought of Tamara's tirade sent a wave of cold anger over my happiness. "I don't know."

It seemed forever before the seats in the theater were all filled, the house lights dimmed, and the performance began. "Here we go," I whispered.

Leanne smiled at me and together we hunkered down to enjoy the performance. Michael was magnificent, of course. His voice was deep and true through each speech. He was so good as the Belligerent Man that the man next to him said, "Hey, buddy, sit down and be quiet. My daughter's in this play. I'd like to be able to hear her."

When he was A Man Among the Dead, I listened to his voice speaking the words of Thornton Wilder. They made me recall many of our courting ritual nights when we were out in some deserted Tallahassee field looking up at the stars and marveling at their mysterious beauty. Michael became like the sailor who "knew them all," and I was again in the safety of his arms facing eternity with him. Tears rolled down my face as he spoke his lines.

I was sure Leanne would think I was just a silly woman to be reacting so, but then I looked over and could make out tears running down her lovely brown face, too. We were soul mates, indeed, I thought. How nice it was that we were able to transcend age to share this wonderful evening.

MARCH

LESSON 28

Finny, his balance gone, swung his head around to look at me for an instant with extreme interest, and then he tumbled sideways, broke through the little branches below and hit the bank with a sickening, unnatural thud. It was the first clumsy physical action I had ever seen him make. With unthinking sureness I moved out on the limb and jumped into the river, every trace of my fear of this forgotten.

A Separate Peace
John Knowles

A ndrew was a handsome young man of medium build and with a light tan color who sat quietly in the back of my classroom. It was as if he almost hid himself behind my fichus tree and hoped I would never call on him. I made the mistake of asking him to describe the character Finny for the class. The embarrassing silence that followed got longer and longer and more and more painful. I made a silent vow never to do that to him again.

I never really knew if I were reaching him with the lessons. He didn't appear to be listening, but then he wasn't talking with others or sleeping. He just had a kind of vacant stare.

He did the assignments I made, but his work was plain and unremarkable. Andrew eluded me.

None of us knew why he suddenly withdrew from school. Most kids who drop out do so by never returning. Andrew went to all the trouble of bringing his parents to school, confronting a horde of counselors and administrators who wanted him to stay, and still had himself removed from the rolls. I often wondered if he were trying in some subtle way to let us know education had failed him somehow, but his quiet withdrawal told us that; not what we could do to help him or improve the system for others.

When he came back to visit me two months later, I was startled to say the least. He stuck his head in the door while I was in my planning period, a giant, friendly grin on his once bashful face.

"Andrew?"

"Hey, Mrs. Webster. Just came by to see how you all were doing without me."

"Well, come in and tell me all about the big, bad world out there."

He hurried in, pulled up a chair, and with a life in his eyes I had never seen in him before, he started talking a mile a minute about his new career.

"You won't believe what I'm doing now. I'm a construction worker on the new Gateway Skyscraper Project, and I'm working the high floors, hard hat and all. I really love it, man. I got all this gear. You wouldn't know me when I'm all duded up. And high!! Ooo, Lord, I get up to twenty stories some days, and I hear we're going to get over thirty stories tall. I tell you, the world looks a whole lot different from up there. I just leave all my problems on the ground. It's like flying, sorta. I feel like an eagle or sea gull or something really graceful. And there are times when it is so peaceful up there. When we break for lunch, I sit out near the edge and think how wonderful and peaceful the world can be so high up there."

I was astounded Andrew could actually talk, and I'm sure my face showed it. Who ever would have imagined him to know so many words? Who would have imagined him to have had such enthusiasm in him? He positively glowed with excitement, and I felt incredibly sad that I never inspired such enthusiasm in him. It still was good to have him there with me, going on and on about the real world and how happy he was to be a part of it.

We talked for another ten minutes, maybe less, when he sort of ran out of steam and needed to move on to say hello to another teacher.

"It's been real good talking to you, Mrs. Webster. Next time you pass downtown, look up, and maybe you'll see me high up waving at ya."

"I'll surely do that, Andrew," I said, reaching over and giving him a hug around the neck. "I'll keep looking up."

Three weeks later on a leisurely Sunday morning, Michael and I sat at our dining table. We were drinking our coffee and perusing the paper.

"Oh, no," Michael said carefully to me across the breakfast table. "Says a former Dunbar student was killed yesterday."

As he folded the section over and turned the paper so I could read it, my heart sank to my toes. I felt a chill flood over me much as a blush spreads over a face. I didn't want to read the story and prayed silently that this student would not be one of mine.

It was Andrew. He had fallen down the elevator shaft from the eighteenth level. He wasn't wearing his safety harness, and they had not yet finished the barriers required every two floors in the shaft so that such an accident could be prevented. For a long time, no one knew Andrew had fallen. He hadn't uttered a sound when it happened. Quiet to the last.

"Oh my God!" is all I remember saying. Then I started to tremble uncontrollably as tears flooded my face. I'd never lost one of my own students to death before. I was thankful at least I found out at home so I wouldn't disgrace myself by carrying on like this at school. I thought I should go on to church, but I couldn't control my tears. I didn't want to have to give explanations to anyone that day. I stayed home instead with Michael, who just held me as we sat on the sofa, and he comforted me until I could function again. The funeral followed a week later, and this funeral I attended. There must have been a thousand people packed into the small sanctuary of the New Jerusalem AME Church on the Eastside. We were shoulder to shoulder in the ancient hardwood pews, and every so often a light-haired head would reveal another white teacher who had come to pay his or her respects to Andrew.

The casket was uncharacteristically closed. I was told that Andrew's body was not recognizable as even human after the fall. Nonetheless, mourners streamed past the casket and touched it and hugged it and fell upon it.

Everyone in the building seemed to be weeping, particularly family members down toward the front. They were letting out loud wails of sorrow and "falling out" into the arms of those strong enough to carry them. This display of raw sorrow was discomforting to me at first. Most white people are taught from early age that tears are unacceptable, especially in adults. I was almost a teenager before I realized grown people could actually cry. It happened when I saw my father break down at the news of his father's death. He just sat down at the dining table and put his head in his arms and sobbed. It was horrifying. It was unnatural.

What Andrew's funeral taught me, though, was that it is natural to feel overwhelmed at the death of someone you love or care about. It is probably more unnatural to hold in all those incredibly painful emotions where they can fester and make you ill in later times. Here in the company of other mourners, I was slowly able to relax and know that I could express myself, and it would be all right. No one would admonish me for my emotion. No one would deny me my feelings.

I let myself feel the loss of Andrew's cheerful face. I let myself feel the incredible emptiness that the death of a young person always brings. I felt his death was such a waste. After all, he had just found himself in this world and knew purpose and joy for the first time. What a tragedy that he could enjoy it for only a short time before he was killed. All that potential gone. All the skyscrapers we may never know.

By the end of the service, which lasted a long time, I was whipped. I had cried more in that one hour than I had in the last three or four years. It was all I could do to get in my car and drive home. There I crawled into bed and slept until the next morning.

When I awoke, I was somehow renewed. The sorrow of the days before had passed. It was replaced by a strange joy—a joy at having known Andrew in the first place and a joy at having had the opportunity to end our relationship well. I went to school a new woman and celebrated life by having a very good teaching day.

LESSON 29

"Ha—lle—lu-jah! Ha—lle—lu-jah!
Ha-lle-lu-jah! Ha-lle-lu-jah! Ha—lle—lu-jah!"

The Messiah
George Handel

It wasn't long after Andrew was buried; I felt sure that it was time for something good to happen. Surely, the winds of fortune had to change and blow a little happiness in Dunbar's direction. One day as I sat in my room grading papers during my planning period, good fortune did smile in the form of Percy when he came to my door and asked if he could talk to me.

"Come on in and have a seat," I said, smiling.

Percy lumbered in and took a chair from one of my tables and pulled it close to my desk. "I heard from an important college this week," he said almost sheepishly. "Been offered a bunch of scholarships to universities near here, but I was waiting for one from Clemson. Well, it finally came."

"Percy!" I cried. "How wonderful!"

I jumped up, went around my desk, and hugged him

around the neck. He endured my affectionate enthusiasm with forbearance.

"What's wrong?" I asked sensing that he wasn't nearly as happy about his achievement as I was.

"I got it wrong," he said.

"You got what wrong?" I asked. "What do you mean?"

He took a deep breath and seemed to be grappling with a weighty problem. "I have let you down, and I don't know how to tell you."

"I doubt that," I assured him. "You're one of my finest students I have ever . . . ."

"No, I'm not. I cheated on your last final. I wasn't prepared like I should have been and when I made an "A" on it you can be sure I didn't earn it myself. I had a cheat sheet and you never saw it in the palm of my hand."

I sat in stunned silence.

"I know it was wrong. I also know it is probably why I got the GPA I needed for the scholarship I've been offered."

"So you've only cheated on your English exam?"

"That's right."

"Well," I said sitting back in my chair with a heavy sigh. "That's quite a revelation."

"I'm really sorry," he said with his eyes cast down to the floor.

Strangely, my heart was suddenly flooded with admiration for this fine young man even as he admitted his wrongdoing. It must have worried him considerably for him to come and confess in this fashion. It was at least a start towards his redemption. It also showed me that he was a lot deeper than many of his counterparts who would not give cheating a second thought. It was, after all, part of "whatever means necessary" to succeed in this world.

"This has been bothering you for a long time, hasn't it?" I finally said.

"I sorta started thinking about it when the scholarship offers started to roll in. I kept thinking that I really didn't deserve them because I didn't earn my English grade honestly. I'm not sure why I can't get on with things. I am just ate up with the guilts."

"Percy," I said, almost smiling at his contrition, "normally, I would be really disappointed to learn something like this, but the fact that you have confessed this to me makes me feel that there's hope for you yet."

I paused here to think through what would be a fair penance. At last it came to me.

"Why don't we make a deal so that you can make amends for your sin and then you will feel like you can move on?"

"All right, what are you thinking?"

"First, you have to give up cheating, no matter how necessary you may think it is. They catch you cheating at Clemson, and you'll be on the next bus home."

"Yes, Ma'am."

"Second, I'm going to assign you an extra book to read, give you an exam on it and then average it into this term's grade. I'll make this exam count 50 percent, so you will have to do well on it to keep your GPA up. If you do poorly on it, that will make your GPA a tiny bit more accurate—making it more level."

"That sounds more than fair to me," he said. "What book would I read?"

"Let me see," I said thoughtfully. "How about *A Tale of Two Cities*? Dickens is a British writer and the book would be a bit of a challenge. Still, it would be worth the effort to get out from under your bad feelings. No?"

He looked at me for a moment and then smiled. "I knew you'd help me out of this dilemma. I feel better already."

After I found him a copy of the book, he hugged my neck and moved on out the door into a better world. I returned to my papers feeling pretty satisfied with my wisdom in handling the matter. There was a knock on my door.

"It's still open, Percy," I said, thinking that he had forgotten something. It was Leanne.

"Hi, may I talk to you?"

"Sure," I said, hoping that my wisdom wasn't again needed for a problem similar to the one she had some months before.

"Guess what? It's going to happen," she said to me. "I'm going to get to go to an Ivy League school. I just found out I have qualified for the National Achievement Award from my PSAT scores. Ms. Parker, my guidance counselor, says I can probably go to college anywhere I want. I'm so excited!"

"Leanne, I am so happy for you!" I embraced her. "How absolutely wonderful this is! Your mother will be so proud. Have you told her yet?"

"No. I wanted you to be the first to know."

Tears began to sting my eyes, but I fought them back. Not today, I told myself. Today was too good for tears.

Just then there was another knock at the door. Rochelle stuck her head in and then entered. She was followed by Yasmina.

"We have something neat to tell you!" Rochelle said. Both girls had big smiles on their faces.

"This is turning out to be quite a day," I said. "Okay, tell me."

"We both have two poems each accepted for the literary magazine for the school," Yasmina said softly.

"Yeah," Rochelle said breathlessly, "the sponsor just told us. Here is my letter of acceptance."

"And here's mine," Yasmina said.

I took the letters and read them quickly. "You guys!" I started hugging each one. "I am so proud of you all!"

"We're pretty proud, too," Rochelle said, "but we're also grateful. Thank you for your help."

"Yes," Yasmina agreed, "thank you."

"Oh, yes," Leanne said. "Thanks so much."

"Ah, you guys," I said as I was being overwhelmed with emotion. "Y'all'd better get out of here before I start to cry or something stupid."

"All right, Mrs. Webster," Leanne said as the three went out the door.

"See you later," Yasmina said.

"Yeah, later," Rochelle said.

I closed the door and savored the joy spreading over me that had eluded me all those weeks after Andrew had died. It was wonderful to feel so happy again.

LESSON 30

Mary Dalton was an odd girl, all right. Bigger felt something over and above the fear she inspired in him. She responded to him as if he were human, as if he lived in the same world as she. And he never felt that in a white person.

But why? Was this some sort of game. The guarded feeling of freedom he had while listening to her was tangled with the hard fact that she was white and rich, and part of the world of people who told him what he could and could not do.

Native Son
Richard Wright

I made a lot of teacher friends during my time at Dunbar. Most of the time we didn't get to see each other except at meetings or on planning days. Most of the time we were garretted in our rooms grading papers, reading ahead in the books from which we teach, and writing up plans that we hoped would inspire and illuminate the youth of our world.

Lydia was, of course, my best friend. From the very moment

she helped me from the restroom that first day—a cowardly mass of Jell-O—she and I had been close. We had many heart-to-heart discussions whenever we would have chance meetings in the lounge during our planning periods. Our lunch periods did not coincide. I would not see her anyway since she ate in the cafeteria, and I usually brought a bag lunch from home.

My lunch companion was Martha Williams, another good friend of mine. She was a white woman at least ten years my senior, who taught remedial reading. She was a matronly sort of person, not too fashion conscious, but hers was a gentle and loving demeanor and she could work miracles with the most deficient of students.

We first got to know each other when we realized that we shared a number of "academically needy" students we were both trying to help. Then, one day we met in the lounge during lunch, and we began making an effort to meet there every day when we could.

One day we were just starting our lunch period together, when another English teacher joined us for the first time. Elizabeth Anne Morley was about as delicate as they come. Just by looking at her fifty-five-year-old white face, her tailored dresses and fine jewelry, I could tell she had undoubtedly been a debutante and a Junior Leaguer in her younger days. She had been married to a CEO of a large local company for twenty-five years when he died unexpectedly and left her with tremendous debt and absolutely no way to support herself. Elizabeth worked hard to get her degree in English education, and she eventually found a job at a private school which paid an insubstantial salary. That is how she eventually came to be teaching at Dunbar.

When she couldn't support herself at a level to which she was accustomed working for the private school, she applied with the county system and got a job in an inner-city school. The closest she'd ever been to black people before was when they worked in her home as domestics, when they bagged her groceries in the grocery store or they served her dinner at the country club. To say the least, Dunbar woke Elizabeth to a whole new reality. Too bad it didn't open her eyes.

"Elizabeth, come join us," Martha said in her typically friendly way, moving her stack of papers to make room for our colleague.

"Thank you," Elizabeth said as she took a seat.

We exchanged pleasantries and complained about the usual nitpicky things that bothered us when she announced, "You know, these children don't smell as I had imagined they might."

Martha's facial muscles did something odd, and my eyes must have twitched because she seemed to sense that her comment was not being well received. Suddenly, Elizabeth began to back track, stuttering and stammering in ways amazing to the ear.

"I mean . . . Well, I was . . . These children are actually quite clean," she continued.

I had to consciously try to keep my mouth from falling open. Martha's eyes seemed to say to me, "What kind of person talks like this any more?"

"I just wish these kids would stop being so lazy," Elizabeth continued. "If they would actually try to learn something, though, they might have a chance. It's just that I have an astounding failure rate this quarter. They just won't do the first thing I ask. Those few who do are so deficient. And some of these people are just plain animals. I just can't seem to get any of them up to an acceptable level."

I know I must have flinched at her use of the word "lazy," and I could see Martha bristle at the term "deficient." The word "animal" was more than either of us could bear. After having been at Dunbar for almost seven months, I had become protective of my students and Martha's tenure here had been even longer. I knew her feelings for these "animals" ran deep. Sure, kids could be very trying at times, but that could be said of any race's children. And people like Elizabeth, with their "petit forte ways" and their superior attitudes, really made me gag.

As a matter of fact, a piece of my sandwich got stuck in my throat, and I began to choke.

"Are you all right?" Elizabeth asked, with an almost insincere concern.

Martha jumped up quickly and began to help me out of the lounge as I coughed and sputtered all the way to the restroom. Once we got there, my airway was clear and both of us started laughing—not just a little, but a lot.

"Can you believe that woman?" Martha laughed through her tears.

"Where do people like her come from?" I laughed back.

"Sweet Jesus, I don't know how she's stayed alive in this area this long harboring all those ill feelings."

"I haven't the faintest idea how she does it."

Once we had exhausted our laughter, we returned to the lounge and, thankfully, Elizabeth had left us.

Fortunately for Dunbar and unfortunately for Elizabeth, she washed out before the year was through. It seemed the more she thought her students behaved like animals, the more they actually did. Finally, it happened. One student turned off the lights to Elizabeth's windowless room, and another student threw a Coke can into the air. The can came down squarely on Elizabeth's head, and that act confirmed what she wanted it to confirm. She quit in a huff and vowed never to deal with "those people" ever again.

We were all pleased.

LESSON 31

People disappeared, reappeared, made plans to go
somewhere, and then lost each other, searched for each other,
found each other a few feet away. Sometime toward midnight
Tom Buchanan and Mrs. Wilson stood face to face discussing
whether Mrs. Wilson had a right to mention Daisy's name.

"Daisy! Daisy! Daisy!" shouted Mrs. Wilson. "I'll say it
whenever I want to! Daisy! Dai—"

Making a short deft movement Tom Buchanan broke
her nose with his open hand.

The Great Gatsby
F. Scott Fitzgerald

In preparing the students for a writing exercise, I chose
several passages from *The Great Gatsby* to be examples for
discussion on how evil manifests itself in characters in the novel.
We talked about how Tom Buchanan had stolen the girlfriend of a
war-bound soldier and married her while the soldier was at war.
Later we would talk about how Daisy had let Gatsby take the
blame for an accident she actually caused. When we talked about

the incident of Tom Buchanan abusing his mistress, Myrtle, there was an audible gasp from the students in my eleventh-grade class.

"What a pig!" I heard Rochelle say from her seat in the front.

"Interesting you should use the term 'pig,'" I said. "'Chauvinist pig' is a term feminists used to use to describe male behavior that was condescending and superior, as Tom truly was toward Myrtle."

"But he's not superior," Rochelle said. "He was rich to begin with and through no power of his own was able just to stay on top. That's not true superiority."

"Tom thinks he's superior, though," I say.

"Yeah," Juanita said. "Remember all that stuff about the book he wanted Nick to read about whites being superior to blacks?"

Heads nodded throughout the class.

"Why does it have to be like that, Ms. Webster?" someone asked me. "Why do some people think they have the right to be over other people?"

"Why do you all ask me 'why' questions like that?" I asked in exasperation. "I'm just an English teacher. I certainly don't know 'why' anything happens, because I am not in charge."

Some random giggles rose and quickly died. I guess the seriousness of the subject calmed any frivolity that was likely to erupt. I also knew abuse was not a stranger to many of the students I taught.

One of the first violent acts I ever witnessed in my life had occurred at Dunbar just a few weeks earlier. A young woman, who had been beaten up by her boyfriend earlier one morning, took a knife to him later that day in the hall right outside my room. I was in the crowd that had gathered after the ruckus, and I was trying to get students back to their classes and away from danger. Although she had only cut his hand, the boy screamed as if he were dying. I am sure she would have silenced him permanently had witnesses not come around and tried to restrain her.

She broke away and as she was leaving the scene of her crime, she suddenly came face-to-face with me. She was the rawest, purest form of anger I had ever seen in a human being. In any being for that matter. Her face was contorted with rage, eyes cut like an animal, jaw set and teeth revealed in a sweaty snarl. "Such is the product of abuse," I thought calmly to myself as she came toward me.

Quite by accident I stood in her path. At the sight of me, the girl froze in her tracks. I froze in mine. "Primitive" and "powerful" were words that flashed into my head as I, oblivious to my own danger, blocked her exit out of the building. I watched as she turned and stomped away in the opposite direction. She was, of course, expelled.

Another memory that came to my mind during our Gatsby discussion was an event I will always remember with extreme fondness. A month or two earlier I had had a very large raspberry sore on my face near my eye. I had gone jogging in my neighborhood, when one of my feet went out from under me, and I fell quite literally on my face. I howled like a banshee as I sat there in the road. I was certain before I looked in a mirror that I'd surely need at least three stitches. By the time I made it home and had a good look at it, I realized it was just a scrape, a large one that stung like crazy.

By the next morning, it scabbed over in a most disgusting manner and because of its strange location and size, I could not cover it with a Band-Aid. It had to sit out there for God and country to see. All eyes were immediately drawn to it, and I could see on the others' faces I was repulsive. I should have stayed home, I thought, but I couldn't afford to stay out for as long as it takes a raspberry to heal. I persevered and pretended the disgusting thing wasn't there at all. Most of the people around me ignored it as well.

I wasn't aware of it at the time, but I had become quite the topic of conversation in a number of places kids hang out—cafeteria, locker rooms and other classes. Lydia had overheard some of the talk, and she came to me to see if I was all right. Some of the kids were sure my husband had "put the mojo" on me. Others of the girls were concerned I might be stuck in an abusive situation, and

I might need help to get out of it. Rochelle had gone to talk to Lydia privately about it and asked her to check up on my life's condition.

"Truly," I assured Lydia. "I quite honestly fell when I was jogging."

"Yeah and I've heard parents say they were just disciplining their children when they accidentally burned them with their cigarettes," she continued.

"Lydia, I promise you Michael is a wonderful husband. Never in all of the years I have known him has he raised so much as an eyebrow at me. Well, maybe an eyebrow. Besides, I wouldn't stay in an abusive relationship like that. Really."

"Well, it does look like you could have scraped yourself in a fall," she said, as she searched my face for clues. "I guess it would be hard for a fist to make such a mark." She then left the room.

At first I was a little put off that Lydia thought I wasn't being honest with her, but then I remembered some of my psych classes saying that many abused women deny vehemently they are being abused. Suddenly, I was touched that she and the students were so concerned about my welfare that they would bother to inquire. I hadn't been teaching at Dunbar a year yet and already I felt like I had a family here.

LESSON 32

Macbeth: So fair and foul a day I have not seen.

Macbeth Act 1, Scene 3
William Shakespeare

Daffodils? I couldn't believe it. I walked into my class early that morning, and there on my desk a pot of brightly blooming daffodils sat. Suddenly I was transported through time back to an Easter in the '70s when I was visiting my maternal grandmother in St. Louis. Her yard was overgrown with a profusion of daffodils and crocus. Yellows and blues—everywhere your eye could look. It was something one doesn't see in Florida, except when the flowers are housed in pots.

Obviously, someone had left these flowers there the afternoon before. My door had been locked when I arrived, and that meant someone had gone to some trouble to leave these for me to find when I first arrived in the morning.

I opened the card that was attached in the few remaining minutes before the bell rang to announce the beginning of the day. It said, "When I see daffodils, I think of you because they are an explosion of cheerfulness, just like you."

As was becoming my normal response, my eyes teared up as I read the name "Mark" at the bottom.

"Bless his little heart," I said in a whisper, wiping back the tears.

"Hope you like 'em," a voice said behind me. I turned and there stood the freckle-faced young man who had been a quiet positive force in my senior class. Mark, the kid who found value in my Emily Dickinson poem, had touched my heart with his insight earlier in the year and presently his sweet gesture was touching my heart again.

"Mark, this is the nicest thing," I said as I hugged him around the neck. "Thank you! Thank you so very much!"

Fortunately for him, the bell rang and he had to leave.

"You're welcome," he said softly. If it had been possible, I am sure I would have seen blushing through his freckles. Awkwardly, he backed away and out the door. "See ya." Then he was gone.

I wasn't sure at that moment if the flowers meant anything more than just a kindness. It was possible Mark had a crush on me. There weren't many lessons on the subject of crushes in college, except to say that they happened. Since teenagers feel things so intensely, teachers need to be careful how they proceed in such matters. Of course, I could have been mistaken. Maybe Mark's flowers were just a gift. Maybe they were no more than a token of appreciation and not affection.

In any event, Mark needed me to be appreciative, but I needed to be sure not to lead him to believe our relationship could be anything more than educational. Even if he was "in love" with me and he was trying to explore his emotions, he had to feel certain that I would never act on it in any way. He needed to feel safe in our relationship, if indeed that was what was going on. I didn't have much time to ponder these things, however. It was time for me to take my position at the door. Even so, as I greeted my students as they came in, my spirits were buoyed up by the token of kindness that sat on my desk for all to see.

"Ooooo, Ms. Webster got a boyfriend!!" some of the students teased.

"Hard to believe, isn't it?" I said with a laugh.

"Yeah, who could believe anybody even likes you?" someone said, but I knew in a heartbeat it was Luscious.

"Who indeed," I responded with a grin. Then it was time to begin the lesson.

As the day passed, my eyes were often drawn to the flowers. They rose so elegantly from my desktop. Lovely yellow bugles on bright green stems. I had decided when it came time for Mark's class to arrive, I would say nothing so he would be spared any embarrassment. But when the time came for his class to arrive, he was not in it. I waited patiently for his arrival—from the counselor's office or from a conference with a college representative. He never came.

The school day ended and still no Mark. I assembled my materials for the nightly lesson preparation/grading session and had to decide whether to take the flowers home to enjoy or leave them there at school to enjoy the next day in the work place. I left the flowers. I wanted them to greet me in the morning and every morning for as long as they would last.

As I was leaving the building, I passed the dean of boys' office, and looking in, I saw Mark sitting there with an angry looking father-figure seated next to him. Mark's clothes were torn and disheveled, and his face was swollen and he had a cut near the mouth. I wanted to go in and see what was wrong, but in the instant he saw me, I saw him glance away quickly, as if he hadn't wanted me to come near. I passed on by toward the teacher mailboxes and found the dean of boys placing yellow copies of referrals in the appropriate teachers' boxes.

"What happened with Mark?" I ask softly, so Mark and the man with him wouldn't hear.

"He got in a fight. Had to suspend him for five days."

"A fight? Mark?" I asked to make sure we were talking about the same person. "I don't believe it."

"Well, believe it. He put a gash in Jonnie Holiday's lip that needed ten stitches."

"Unbelievable! You don't know what it was about, do you?"

"Had to do with some girl he gave flowers to this morning. Seems Jonnie was making fun of him about it and the girl, and Mark just lost it."

My heart sank to the pit of my stomach. Mark was defending my honor, or his honor concerning me. My lovely day suddenly turned very dark as a sadness that was hard to describe descended upon it. I remembered a time when I was in the third grade when some older boys found a love note I had written to Harry Stafford. They were reading it aloud in a mock female voice to a large crowd on the playground. All I could do was skulk away and hide behind the library until recess was over. Their abuse hurt me so badly that I could have died right there on the spot. Sadly, I never felt the same about good old Harry, either.

Perhaps this was a similarly disagreeable event for Mark. I wouldn't have been surprised if I had already begun to slip from his immediate concern. I easily could relate to that.

I went home that night and felt a dull sorrow as I pondered Mark's dilemma. After a great deal of thought, I wrote a thank-you note and mailed it the next day to his home where he could not possibly be shamed in front of his peers. I chose not to mention the fight, and I left him with the assurance that I would always appreciate his thoughtfulness.

It seemed to reassure him. By the time Mark's suspension was over, the flowers, still on my desk, were just beginning to fade. I had left them there for everyone, including Mark, to see how proud I was of them.

APRIL

LESSON 33

Shall I compare thee to a summer's day?
Thou are more lovely and more temperate:

"Sonnet 18"
William Shakespeare

I f I had to use one word to describe Thanh Mai, it would
have to be "sunny." She was by far the most cheerful person
I had ever met in my life. She always had a smile on her face, even
when she was unaware that it was being observed. I'd look up
during a reading assignment or during an exam, and the faintest
glimmer of a smile played on her lips. She was astounding.

This happiness was all the more impressive when I took
into account the fact she was an Amer-Asian. I had never asked
her directly, but she had talked about going to Korea to visit
relatives, so I assumed her parents met while her father served
in the military.

She was a physically lovely child. Her face was decidedly
Oriental, with almond eyes and round face. Her raven black hair
was also coarse, long, and straight. She usually kept it pulled back

tightly in a bun. Her skin was soft and a creamy yellow brown. Her lips were very full and, as I've said, always curving into a smile. She did take her share of abuse for her racial composition, though. Robert was one student who constantly called her names, and when I'd fuss at him about it he'd always say he was just kidding.

"You half-breed, ashy Haitian," he called across the room to Thanh Mai one day.

"Robert, I'm going to put you out of here if you don't stop talking like that," I almost yelled. His unkindness, especially after he had just announced he was preaching a sermon next Sunday at his ever-so-Christian church, was all the more offensive to me.

"I'm just kidding, Mrs. Webster. Really. I actually like Thanh Mai a lot," Robert said.

"Well, you could have fooled me. Now, you just confine your comments to the text and we'll all be very happy. Do you understand me?"

I then gave him one of my better-watch-out looks, and he slunk down into his desk chair for the remainder of the class.

"Okay," he said, suddenly sheepish.

When class was over, I pulled Thanh Mai aside to talk with her about what had just transpired.

"Thanh Mai, does it bother you for Robert to be so . . ."

"Oh, Mrs. Webster, Robert is really quite harmless," she said, smiling her incredibly wonderful smile. "I just pay him no never-mind."

"Well, you're a bigger person about it than I would be," I said. "It just steams me to hear him talk like such a hypocrite. One minute he's talking about loving and serving Jesus. Then in the same breath, he's persecuting someone. I can hardly stand it sometimes."

"Mrs. Webster, don't you worry about me. I can take it. You see, I think I understand Robert. He doesn't mean to hurt me. He thinks I like the attention. It's kinda like 'ranking' or 'playing the dozens.'"

"Playing the dozens?" I asked.

"My father told me that in slave times, those slaves who had deformities or who were too old to work or too young to do anything useful, were sold by the dozen. So these slaves invented this 'dozens' game to help them learn to take verbal abuse. They were the 'least of the least,' and they could expect a tremendous amount of sorrow in their lifetime. The object of the game was for one slave to make a more outlandish insult than the one before him. Robert doesn't really mean half of what he says. He's just trying to out-do me."

"But I've never heard you try to insult him."

"I'm not really very good at the game, Mrs. Webster. I guess that is why I don't play."

I thought maybe she didn't play because she knew how badly it could hurt a person, but I decided to take her word for it.

"Really, Mrs. Webster, if I thought Robert meant what he says, it probably would hurt me. But believe me, his abuse is mild compared to what I got in Korea."

"Really?"

"If my father hadn't been in the military, we would have been forced to live in a really low-rent section of Seoul. Blacks are horribly persecuted in Korea. And forget mixed children. We're totally outcast. I had rocks thrown at me, and even though I don't know a lot of Korean, I knew enough to know when I was being insulted. No, for me, America is a tiptoe through the park compared to Korea, and Robert is laughable most of the time."

"You are an extraordinary person, Thanh Mai," I said, looking over her wonderful, gentle face.

"You're not half-bad yourself, Mrs. Webster," she smiled as she turned to leave for her next class.

LESSON 34

He ran like a blind man. Two or three times he fell down.
Once he knocked his shoulder so heavily against a tree that
he went headlong. Since he had turned his back upon the
fight, his fears had been wondrously magnified. Death about
to thrust him between the shoulder blades was far more
dreadful than death about to smite him between the eyes.
When he thought of it later, he conceived the impression
that it is better to view the appalling than to be merely
within hearing. The noises of the battle were like the stones;
he believed himself liable to be crushed.

The Red Badge of Courage
Stephen Crane

There was a page about it in the teacher handbook issued
me during the early weeks of school. It had undoubtedly
been written during the late '60s when riots in schools were
commonplace, and there actually was a page dedicated to riot
procedure. The first thing a teacher was supposed to do was pull as
many breathing bodies into the classroom as he or she physically

could and then close the door. It didn't matter whether these students belonged to the given teacher or not. The purpose of removing the students from the hall was to remove as many people from harm's way as was possible so "a volatile situation can be defused as quickly as possible."

These words came to my mind as it suddenly occurred to me one day between classes that a riot was indeed happening. It began with a few screams and a few students rushing by in a panic.

Since it was not unknown for students to occasionally run past me in the hall, it took me a few minutes before I realized something was very wrong. Soon everyone was running and screaming, and that's when I began fishing for students. Like a seine net, my arms would envelop a kid and quickly and jerkily usher him or her into my classroom. I caught maybe eight kids along with my regular students who had rushed into the room frantically.

When the halls were almost cleared, I could just make out Roscoe. He staggered forward toward me like a drunken man, one of his arms pressed to his chest by the other. As he came closer I could see a wild, crazy look on his face. His mouth hung open, and he gasped for breath as if he had been running a marathon.

I started to go toward him to collect him into my "school of fish" when he veered awkwardly down a hall that ran perpendicular to mine. It was then I realized what had caused the commotion. Roscoe had been shot. Unlike in the movies, this gunshot wound didn't exactly bleed blood. It never occurred to me before that more than blood vessels are damaged in a gunshot wound. There was all manner of fluid and tissue in a trail Roscoe left behind as he stumbled his way to the front office.

I was horrified when I realized what it really was on the floor and a thrill of fear ran through my body. A gun and gunman were, as far as I knew, still on campus, possibly pursuing Roscoe. That meant that he or she might come flying down that hall at any moment. I rushed back to my classroom, locked the door, then pulled it shut to protect all of us inside.

Finally, the sound of sirens bled through the walls and mingled with the sobs and heavy breathing of the students in my classroom. "Did anybody see what happened?" I finally asked.

"I saw it, Ms. Webster," Mark said. "Elliot Smith pulled a gun from his book bag and just plain shot Roscoe. Right there in the courtyard. Right there during the second lunch period. I was standing right next to him, too. Damn! I could be dead now!"

"Me, too," Vermellia said with a great sob, and then putting her head in fretful hands she screamed, "Sweet Jesus! I could be lying on the cold, cold ground right this very minute!"

"Where was Roscoe hit?" I asked. I hadn't been able to tell clearly when he was in the hall. He was after all clutching his chest. Nobody could answer me. Most had just heard the gun go off and they fled without any looking back.

Sobs from a few other girls around the room became louder and more pronounced. All faces, including mine, I'm sure, had wild looks on them, and I could almost hear every heart pounding loudly. Fortunately, the intercom clicked on and the principal's voice addressed us.

"Students and teachers. Please remain in your classrooms until further notice."

"He's still loose!" Vermellia screamed, and her sobs began once again only this time she was louder.

"Vermellia, please calm down," I said softly, moving toward her to offer a hug, a hand or any comfort she'd take.

"But, Miss Webster, I almost died! That bullet could have hit me!"

"But it didn't, Vermellia," I assured her. "You are safe now. The door's locked. We will stay here until the office tells us different. We're all going to do just fine," I said in as calming a tone as I could muster under the circumstances.

"You don't think bullets can come through doors, Miss Webster?" she sobbed.

"No one is going to shoot anybody." I was even starting to get nervous now. Vermellia was unsettling everyone, including me, and I was afraid she would get everyone so agitated and frightened, that a mini-riot might break out inside my room. I wished the office would give us more information about what had happened and what was presently going on, but I imagined there was tremendous chaos up there right now. I was just as glad to be in a classroom.

"All right, class! Everybody listen up!" I said with an amazing authority. "I want each of you to have a seat. That's it. That's it. Everybody just calm down."

Vermellia started to open her mouth to scream, when I overrode her voice with my own.

"Everybody sit up straight! That's good. Yes. There we go. Now, put your feet flat on the floor. Good. Good. That's it. Now, everybody, I want you to close your eyes. Come on, now. Everybody! Do it!"

I walked around the room checking to see that everyone was complying. When I was reasonably sure they were, I took a seat myself and began the yoga lesson.

"Now, I want everyone to take one deep breath."

"What?" one of the strange students I had "reeled in" asked.

"Just do it," I snapped.

I could hear the deep inhalations throughout the room and was hoping this little exercise would help relieve the tension that was in there.

"Now. We're going to take another deep breath, only this time we're going to hold it in for the count of four and let it out for the count of eight. Understand?"

There were no questions, and I was actually rather surprised that the group was so amenable to my suggestions. Under ordinary circumstances, I'd have gotten a lot of grief about such an activity. It pleased me to know I was helping in some small way. I felt powerful and yet terrified because these children were looking to me to help them cope with the situation.

"Breathe in," I said. "Two, three, four. Hold, two, three, four. Out, two, three, four, five, six, seven, eight. Again."

I could hear the breaths going in and out appropriately. I imagined the tension was slowly melting, and I was right. We continued in this way for another five or six breaths and before too long, a laugh rose into the air. Then more laughing began to move through the room. Some of the students had begun talking. Others gossiped about trivial things. Still others soon asked if they might turn on the television, and I let them. Only Vermellia was inconsolable. She cried quietly at her desk until there was a knock at the door.

We all froze and fell silent at the sound. I walked up to the door carefully.

"Yes?" I asked it.

"Is Vermellia Feldman in there?"

"Why?" I asked.

"Her mother is here to take her home."

I opened the door a crack and could see an office aide with pass and a distraught older woman standing next to her.

"Vermellia, your mama's here."

Quickly she gathered up her things and hurried out the door where she collapsed into the arms of her waiting mother. I wondered how the mother knew to come. Maybe, I thought, our breathing exercises had carried a telepathic message from her daughter to her. Later, I discovered that after the shooting had occurred, one or two children got to the pay phones to call home. Before the hour was up, the entire neighborhood buzzed with the information, and parents by the hundreds swamped the doors of the school.

Roscoe lived. He had only been shot through the forearm. He may have been one of the most handsome guys in any of my classes, but he proved to have been somewhat of a bully. He had, for some reason, made it his mission to torment a poor little freshman every day for the first half of the year. I actually found all of this hard to believe because Roscoe had always been a gentleman in my class. I guess looks can be deceiving.

He allegedly said things like "Give me your money or I'll beat you up." "Bring me my lunch or I'll beat you up." "Your girlfriend looks like a 'ho,' now let me beat you up." To me, these words did not sound like they belonged to Roscoe.

When the freshman had had abuse up to his eyebrows, he brought his mother's gun to school in his book bag, and when Roscoe started his usual harassment, the freshman pulled out the revolver, took aim, and fired. Roscoe was lucky to be alive as were the fifty children who were standing near him in the lunchroom. The poor little freshman was not so lucky. He would spend a week in jail, untold time in a juvenile facility, and he would be expelled from the county schools for the rest of his life. If it weren't already, his life was now surely to be in peril. He and his family would be wise to move out of the state.

Of course, the next day, we had a gun search. Armed with metal detectors and ammo sniffing dogs, a staff of twenty-five administrators from the central office searched everyone and everything at Dunbar Senior High. It did seem a little bit after-the-fact to me. "The cow was already out of the barn," as they say. It did not surprise me that no weapons of any kind were found. It was also no surprise that life went on as always.

What did surprise me was my reaction to the danger. I had been cool. I had behaved in a most professional manner. Fear didn't come to me until late that night, when I realized I could have been in the line of fire had the freshman continued to pursue his target. I shivered a bit at the thought and was thankful my students had only seen me in complete control of the situation. It was quite a miracle, actually.

LESSON 35

The wind came back with triple fury, and put out the light for the last time. They stay in company with the others in other shanties, their eyes straining against crude walls and their souls asking if He meant to measure their puny might against His. They seemed to be staring at the dark, but their eyes were watching God.

Their Eyes Were Watching God
Zora Neale Hurston

Florida is one of the finest places in the world to live and work. It has been my home all of my life, and I can imagine no other place in the universe where I could be as happy. The summers can be extremely hot and humid, but I have always loved that feeling of a steam room or sauna. The winters can still be pretty chilly on occasion. I can remember a Gator Bowl game where I sat shivering in 11-degree winter weather and that didn't include the wind chill factor, which had to be considerable. Also, Floridians have no idea how to cope with the cold. Our houses are poorly insulated against it, our heaters are not proper furnaces, and our clothes are usually flimsy and much too light to keep us warm. But that doesn't matter. The cold days do not occur often. What does occur quite frequently is the thunderstorm. It doesn't take much humidity or heat to get one of those monsters cranking. All it takes is a mass of cool air and a mass of warm, humid air and we're in the thunderstorm business.

In my education classes I was taught that weather has a tremendous effect on children at school. There seems to be a direct correlation between the weather outside and the emotional state of the class inside. Rain can either whip the students into a frenzy or lull them to sleep. Windy weather can energize a group of kids as it enlivens the air. Freezing temperatures can make children more playful, but if the heater overcompensates for the cold, the warmth can put everybody to sleep. A thunderstorm, however, does something to us that is unlike the effect of any other form of weather. A thunderstorm awakens truly primal fears in us. Add to that the threat of a tornado, and we feel Oz looming just over the horizon.

One such storm front approached Jacksonville during the spring of that year. As I drove to work that morning, the humidity was high, and it was uncomfortably warm even for a spring morning. I ran the air conditioner of my car all the way to work. I didn't really give the gathering clouds much thought, since I had witnessed hundred of these storms before. I just carried on as I usually do when a storm threatens—I seek shelter. When I arrived at Dunbar, I parked my car and hurried inside the school building.

After about an hour or so, I had forgotten about the impending weather. I was busy proceeding with my day. I couldn't tell that the clouds were banking in dangerous formations outside since all I had for a window in my classroom was the tall, 12-inch-wide, rectangular Plexiglas slit at the back of the room. I could only be slightly aware of any weather changes with such a window.

By the time my second-period class convened, however, the atmosphere outside the school was most volatile. At first I became aware of vague rumblings outside which I mistook for booming bass speakers of a passing car.

"They sure are tuning up for a concert," I said as I looked up from the roll book.

"That's thunder, Mrs. Webster," Joshua, who was sitting in the back and near the window, told me.

"No way," Robert said.

"Yes, way," Joshua fired back. "It's like night over to the east."

I got up from my seat and went to the window slit. Even through the translucent plastic, I could see the ominous shape of the rising storm, the split sky with the dark top and white bottom. I could also see pieces of color and shape swirling and dancing around in circles just beyond the plastic barrier. I could just make out a soft whining sound as the wind passed by.

"Tornado," I whispered to myself, and I felt the fear rise from the pit of my stomach.

I tried to remember what one was to do if a tornado ever rumbled through. If we had a cellar or a basement, we could all go down in it and be safe, but in Florida, where the water table is just inches below the top soil, there are no cellars. You're supposed to get in your bathtub or stand in a doorway. Or is that what you're supposed to do in an earthquake? I wasn't sure.

My hope was that it was just another passing storm which would expend its fury in an hour and be gone. I went back to my desk and continued to call the roll.

"Class, please open your books and turn to page . . ."

The lights suddenly sputtered out, and from far away a cheer of delight went up. My students immediately joined in the happy noise as we sat in the incredibly dark classroom.

"All right, now," I said in my most authoritative voice, "you've been in the dark before, children. Calm down. Everything is going to be all right."

About this time the emergency light went on and cast its garish illumination upon us all.

Of course, it wasn't enough light by which to read. My lesson was suspended for the moment.

"Mrs. Webster!" a girl cried, "Samuel just grabbed my bootie!"

"I did not!" Samuel protested from the opposite side of the room. "I'm way over here!"

"Whoever is bothering his neighbor needs to stop right now!" I said lamely.

"Quit!" she yelled.

With great exasperation, I got up from my desk and started to move toward the wronged female when a not-too-distant explosion shook the building. The emergency light went off and silence fell over the group. I stopped dead in my tracks, not knowing what else to do. I waited.

The next sound we heard was a ripping kind of noise which got louder and louder. I could just barely make out the forms of my students, and I don't know whether it was my imagination, but I could have sworn I could see their wide, frightened eyes. I can only guess what they saw when they looked at me.

Next came a horrible pressure to the ears. Then came a roaring that sounded like a train rushing at us. We couldn't hear our screams. The Plexiglas of my window slit had probably not been properly replaced after the great robbery in February, because it suddenly exploded inward and struck Joshua's raised arm protecting his head. He fell violently onto the floor next to his desk. I tried to rush over to him, but I was in a dream state—a slow-motion nightmare where my legs couldn't move fast enough either to escape danger or save the one who needed saving.

Students scrambled frantically under their desks and a few dived under the table in the back. My heart beat wildly as I practically crawled toward Joshua. As I stooped down beside him, I saw a deep gash on his forehead. With the skirt of my dress, I applied pressure to stop the bleeding. In my mind the lectures on AIDS replayed themselves. "Never touch a bleeding wound without the appropriate rubber gloves."

I ignored the mental replay and kept applying pressure to his wound. I couldn't let Joshua bleed to death. His groans were just barely audible over the rushing, roaring sounds that filled my classroom. Paper and books flapped through the air like manic birds. It was horrible.

Slowly the roaring started to die down, only to be replaced by the sobbing of frightened girls and the heavy breathing of stunned boys. Suddenly, the emergency light came back on and then, after a few disoriented seconds, we heard the crackle of the intercom as the principal came on to give us direction.

"We're not absolutely sure, but we have been hit by some extreme weather. Please stand by."

"No, duh," I said softly to myself.

Slowly the students got up and moved back to their seats and tried to reorganize their belongings that had been scattered all about the room.

Several students and I propped Joshua up against the wall. He and I both sat in a considerable pool of blood. I tried to comfort him as best I could. He seemed a bit befuddled and confused.

"Room 409?" a voice on the intercom asked.

"Yes," I said to the air.

"Do you have an emergency?"

"Yes!" I cried. "I have a bleeding head injury and a lot of kids who are pretty shaken up."

"Hold on. Help is on the way."

Through the loud torrents of rain that now poured through the window, sirens from the nearby fire station could be heard in the distance. The sound of help on its way flooded me with relief. Suddenly and most inappropriately, I started thinking about going to the store after school to buy some color-safe bleach to get the bloodstain out of my dress. My dress was probably ruined, but it was important at that moment that I try to save it. Strange how the mind protects itself by thinking about the trivial when heavy matters are occurring.

Before too many minutes, office and rescue personnel were in the room administering first aid to Joshua, who was eventually removed on a stretcher and taken to the hospital for observation. He required seven stitches and a tetanus shot, but he had quite a story to tell his friends. He was the only medical emergency to come from this school.

The neighborhood was not so lucky. It seems a tornado had touched down at three different locations in the immediate area. Five small houses had been literally overturned and fourteen people required hospitalization. Thankfully, there were no fatalities.

School was canceled for the rest of the day since there was only emergency power. Also, many children were frantic to get home and check on family and seek the comfort of Mama. As soon as bus transportation could be arranged, the kids left. Hysterical parents had already made it to the school—some of them on foot and others by car—to be sure their children were safe and well.

Another dramatic moment came later, after the building was cleared of children. As I walked down the hall to attend an emergency faculty meeting, still wearing my blood-stained dress, I had to pass the library. My eyes beheld what looked like a bombed out building. A wall of windows had blown inward and the rows of bookcases stood silhouetted against the now clear, blue sky.

Of course, almost every book had been blown off its shelf. The librarian stood dazed in a fluttering heap of paper carnage.

"We'll just have to clean all this up," she said to no one particular. "We'll just have to get it cleaned up."

Our meeting was held in the cafeteria since there was no longer a usable library. Mr. Ward informed us that a freak tornado had hit us, and there had been little warning. What warning there was didn't allow us enough time to evacuate the children. As it was, keeping the students in the rooms was the best thing. Knots of excited conversation traveled throughout the room marveling at the event and how lucky we were to have so few injuries. We were then dismissed to go home and rest and prepare for the next day's clean up.

As I arose to leave, Ms. Weller came over to me and looked me up and down.

"I hope you wore gloves when you rendered aid to that child."

"I didn't have any gloves on me," I said.

"You know you have violated school board policy, don't you?" she said with an irritated, official tone.

"Yes, ma'am," I answered, feeling a real panic rise from the pit of my stomach, "but I had to help him. He was hurt pretty badly, and I couldn't just let him bleed there."

"Yes, you could have. He wasn't going to die. And now you have exposed yourself to a potential hazard. How do you know for sure that he didn't have AIDS?"

"I didn't know. Why? Does he?"

"Not to my knowledge, but there is a child with AIDS in one of your classes. You very easily could have been contaminated had that child been injured."

I was suddenly breathless. "Who in my class has AIDS?"

"It is against the privacy laws for me to tell you that, but in the future, you get some gloves and use them in your next emergency. You never know anymore. You better go have a blood test."

For the first time, I was really scared for my own life. The fact I had survived a tornado was truly remarkable, but after the dean had spoken to me, I was far more nervous than I had ever been during the worst of the storm. I went home in an absolute daze, and I wouldn't let Michael near me without appropriate protection until I tested negative twice for the HIV or AIDS I might have contracted.

For some time after, I had trouble dealing with the idea that someone was dying before my very eyes, and I didn't know who it was. It made me nuts to know I couldn't reach out to that person, figuratively or literally. I did go out and buy some surgical gloves that next week so I could keep a supply in the drawer of my desk, but I prayed I'd never need them again, and hoped I'd have the courage to deal bravely with the death of yet another student when the time came.

LESSON 36

Then they were old. Their bodies honed, their odor sour. Squatting in a cane field, stooping in a cotton field, kneeling by a river bank, they had carried a world on their head. They had given over the lives of their own children and tendered their grandchildren. With relief they wrapped their heads in rags, and their breasts in flannel; eased their feet into felt. They were through with lust and lactation, beyond tears and terror. They alone could walk the roads of Mississippi, the lanes of Georgia, the fields of Alabama unmolested. They were old enough to be irritable when they chose, tired enough to look forward to death, disinterested enough to accept the idea of pain while ignoring the presence of pain. They were in fact at last free.

The Bluest Eye
Toni Morrison
Copyright 1970
Reprinted with permission of International
Creative Management Group, Inc.

When I first spoke with Mrs. Harris, we were on the phone. I had been summoned to the faculty lounge to take her call, and it was all I could do to hear over the din of teacher conversations.

"You'll have to speak a little louder, Mrs. Harris," I said to her, straining to hear her raspy words on the other end.

"I'm Robert Perkins' grandmother," she said, and I thought I could detect a bit of irritation in her voice. It was hard to tell because of the noise. "I just got your letter about Robert and his behavior. Just what do you mean by 'disruptive' and 'unkind'?"

"Mrs. Harris, Robert is a very nice kid when he wants to be, but he cuts up in my class all the time. He talks constantly, even when I've asked him to be quiet. And he has a tendency to try to get me off the subject by asking religious questions of me. Not that I object to religion, it's just that we have other things to discuss, and we don't need to get off track. He can also be a bit brutal to the other students."

I thought of the way he treated Joshua. And how mercilessly he treated Thanh Mai.

"Sometimes his behavior borders on the disrespectful, not only to me but to other students as well."

"Meaning?" There was no doubt this time she was angry.

"I mean that Robert consciously tries to put people down in front of the class. One day he even called me and my assignments 'stupid' and that I was 'crazy' to think high school students should have to do stuff like that."

"Just what did you ask them to do?"

At this point my throat became dry, and I could feel a trembling coming over my voice. I resented anyone thinking I'd have students doing anything that was not School Board approved or educationally sound. This grandmother, however, definitely felt teachers quite capable of asking the "stupid" or "crazy," so maybe Robert came by his attitudes honestly.

"All I asked the class to do was read a short story in their literature book silently and then answer the questions on a work sheet I had given them."

"And that's all you asked them to do?"

"Mrs. Harris, I try to be very reasonable and fair about my assignments. I don't give busy work. Every assignment is designed to lead to the next one. Besides, I have been very patient with Robert. I've given him plenty of time to turn himself around, but he still misbehaves, and I don't ever need to be called 'stupid' or 'crazy' by anybody. I have always treated Robert with kindness and respect, and I feel I deserve the same."

"Well, I want you to know, Mrs. Webster, I do not tolerate misbehavior or disrespect to any teacher. All teachers deserve respect whether they are stupid or not, and I'll guarantee Robert will not be a problem for you ever again."

I don't believe she meant to be insulting and for that reason, I let her "stupid or not" comment pass.

"Well, thank you for your help, Mrs. Harris," I said as nicely as I could. "I really appreciate your call."

I hung up the phone, and Coach Gleason, who had overheard my side of the conversation, said, "I hate parent calls. It's like we're such a bunch of idiots or something. And they always believe the kid over us. Don't they know their kids will lie?"

"Maybe that's why they call," I offered. "To get the facts straight."

"Oh, no. They call to intimidate. The old 'I-pay-your-salary trick.' God, I hate parent calls."

I felt about the same way, but at least this one was over, and I was much better once I had a cola to soothe my dry, trembly voice.

The next day during my first-period class as I stood in front of the room explaining the next activity, there was a strong knock at the door. Since I was closest to the door, I went to answer it so I could more quickly get back to my explanation.

I opened the door and there stood an ancient, brown woman carefully dressed in her church clothes, I imagined. She was heavily wrinkled and stooped with age. Still, she wore a pillbox hat that matched her pink dress, and she clutched a little pink purse that matched her pink shoes. She smelled of talc and toilet water, and it was apparent she had taken great care in dressing. With Robert at her side, his head down and his eyes avoiding mine, I knew this must be Mrs. Harris.

"May we come in?" she asked.

"Of course," I said, opening the door wide to accommodate her as she painfully shuffled in. "Is there something I can do for you?" I asked once they were both inside.

"No, Mrs. Webster," she said, "but there is something Robert can do for you."

"But, Grandma . . ." Robert said softly and nervously to her, trying to pull her aside to speak further. He didn't get to finish his sentence, because she gave him such a look that had it been given to me, I would have melted into a small greasy spot on the floor.

"Now!" she said.

"Yes, Grandma."

Robert went to the front of the class, just in front of my desk and stood. His head was bowed and his hands were folded in front of him.

"Mrs. Webster, I want to apologize to you for my bad behavior in class and calling you 'stupid' and 'crazy.' Class, I want to apologize to you for taking valuable education time away from you. Grandma, I want to apologize to you for shaming you this way, and, Jesus, I apologize to You for falling from Your ways and Your teachings. Amen."

The class sat there as stupefied as I was. I had never seen such a public act of contrition before, and I didn't know how to react.

Finally, I said, "I accept your apology, Robert, and I am sure that the class accepts your apology as well. And thank you, Mrs. Harris. Thank you, both."

The old woman nodded and then painfully moved to the door. I followed to see her and Robert safely down the hall and out the building. When I returned to the class, there was loud chattering and discussion going on.

"Hey, Mrs. Webster, who was that?" Rochelle asked.

"That was Robert Perkins," Juanita answered. "He goes to my church."

"But, why was he apologizing to our class?" Harold asked. "He's never been in here before."

"Oh, he's in my second period class, and he's just practicing for a play he's going to be in," I said almost without thinking. I hate lying because I always seem to get caught in my lies, but Robert had suffered enough that day, and I saw no reason to expose him to any more humiliation, especially to a group that didn't even know him very well. His gesture was sufficient, and sure enough, he never gave me or another student a moment's problem for the rest of the year.

LESSON 37

He was dressed like a ragpicker. There were only a few faded hairs left on his bald skull and very few teeth in his mouth, and his pitiful condition of a drenched great-grandfather had taken away any sense of grandeur he might have had. His huge buzzard wings, dirty and half plucked, were forever entangled in the mud. They looked at him so long and so closely that Pelayo and Elisenda very soon overcame their surprise and in the end found him familiar. Then they dared to speak to him, and he answered in an incomprehensible dialect with a strong sailor's voice. That was how they skipped over the inconvenience of the wings and quite intelligently concluded that he was a lonely castaway from some foreign ship wrecked in the storm. And yet, they called in a neighbor woman who knew everything about life and death to see him, and all she needed was one look to show them their mistake.

"He's an angel," she told them . . . .

"A Very Old Man with Enormous Wings"
Gabriel Garcia-Marquez

M r. Ward, my principal, was not a hard man to
understand. He was in his late fifties, his close-cropped
hair was graying and he was extremely tall. His dark skin was
leathery from having served so many years outside as a football and
track coach. Before he arrived at Dunbar some fifteen years before
I did, he had been the athletic director of a neighboring school.
He was a neighborhood tradition with which to be reckoned.

He seemed to live his life as if it were a football game,
constantly using sports analogies to explain the things he wanted
us teachers and the students to do. He always wanted the teachers
to try new strategies and plays to see what would help the students
"win their way toward the touchdown of success." This tendency
toward sports metaphor could be trying on those of us who hated
high school gym and all activities that smacked of exertion and
sweat. Mr. Ward, however, had a host of "game plans" he wanted
us to try, and most of us "played" along.

I wasn't always as enthusiastic as I needed to be about some of
his ideas. His "Stop! Drop! and Give-Me-Twenty-Minutes-of-
Reading Week" was a bit much. At any time during the day,
someone could get on the intercom and announce, "Stop! Drop!
and Read!" At that moment, regardless of the planned academic
activity, the teacher and students were to get out a book, magazine
or newspaper and read any part. Then, some minutes later, a voice
would announce that we could "Resume normal activity." It
reminded me of movies I had seen where a drill sergeant would
demand 100 push-ups of a recruit at any given moment for any
reason.

Far be it from me to discourage reading at any time, but it is
hard to switch gears from compound-complex sentences to comic
book exploits. But I did try to "go the distance," at least, no matter
the activity. I was new to the education game so maybe I could
learn from all these activities. I'd never know if I didn't try.

Mr. Ward was not what you would call a friendly man. He
never seemed to let us know if we teachers were doing what he

wanted us to do. Most of the faculty meetings became gripe sessions about how our halls were dirty and our desks needed scrubbing. We were "failing our young people," when we didn't make them behave or if we let them get away with wrong-doing. After a few months, I began to tune him out, because I knew I would never please him.

I have this theory about criticism. If it is unrelenting, it becomes useless. Parents think if they harp on a kid about his dirty room, then he will clean it. Teachers think if they tell a kid he has 47 errors in a written passage, then he will improve his spelling and grammar. Principals think if they tell a faculty they aren't helping enough kids, then they will teach better. Unfortunately, life doesn't work that way. If criticism really made people better, then Dunbar should have the best faculty in the universe. Its students would have been attending the Ivy Leagues more frequently.

I was complaining to Michael one evening over dinner about how hard it was to please Mr. Ward, and Michael opened my eyes to an intriguing notion.

"He reminds me of my ninth-grade gym teacher, Mr. Wilson. He thought the best way to motivate people was to make them mad. Then, they'd run out and try to prove him wrong."

I thought about that for a minute. "That really is interesting," I said. "Maybe all Mr. Ward is trying to do is make us mad so we'll go prove him wrong by becoming better teachers. You may be onto something."

From that day forward, I tried to look at Mr. Ward as nothing more than the ninth-grade gym teacher my husband had. It helped a lot. Mr. Ward's gruff criticisms became almost comical in my mind. His reverse psychology was no longer effective with me. Then something happened that made me see that I still don't know all there is to know about people.

One day, I noticed a nest full of baby pigeons in a roof joist. It had become an unsightly mess from weeks of droppings and loose feathers. It made me recall a day when I was a little girl. My mother and I had taken a bus downtown to do some shopping, and I was intrigued with the pigeons that bobbed and waddled everywhere we went. I tried with all my might and energy to catch one.

"Pigeons are just rats with wings," my mother said as she discouraged me from trying to touch even a feather. That memory sprang to mind when I spied the nest and its nasty, chirping cargo. Mr. Ward must have heard this old saying as well because he came up behind me, saw what I was looking at, and promptly summoned the custodian to come and remove the filth from the premises.

I felt horrible. I felt somehow responsible for the demise of a generation of little pigeons who through no fault of their own were filthy. It was their nature to be gross, so why should they be destroyed?

The bell rang, so I didn't have much time to be remorseful. I had classes to teach and a whole set of life problems that needed my immediate attention. The pigeon babies were forgotten.

After school, I had a department meeting to attend. I had two sets of papers I wanted to grade completely, and I needed to sweep my classroom. It was well after five before I started to move out of the building. I was one of the last faculty members in the building.

I was in the hall, just passing by Mr. Ward's office, when I saw his door was partly ajar. In order to be polite, I put my head in the door to say good night, when I caught him in the act—he was dropper feeding the lot of pigeon babies I had thought he was going to execute earlier in the day.

He turned and appeared to try to block my view of the babies, but the chirping told me clearly what was behind him.

"Mr. Ward, you old softie," I said, with a smile.

He had a rather sheepish expression on his face which hardened into a glare. "That fact will never leave this room, will it, Mrs. Webster?"

"No, sir. It never will," I said, turning to go. I laughed aloud all the way to my car, and for the rest of that night, the thought of Mr. Ward and the pigeons brought a smile to my face.

LESSON 38

Then the fish came alive, with his death in him, and rose high out of the water showing all his great length and width and all his power and beauty. He seemed to hang in the air above the old man in the skiff. Then, he fell into the water with a crash that sent spray over the old man and over all of the skiff.

The Old Man and the Sea
Ernest Hemingway

Whenever I read this passage, I see Harold, a football-playing fool who was well over 6 feet and must have weighed 250. He, like so many others on the team, was enormous, and he played defensive end. It was a good thing that Harold was on the Viking squad because it kept him off the streets and out of trouble. The coaches were also there to keep an ever-watchful eye on him. He was sure to get a scholarship if he didn't sabotage himself before he could be recruited. He was, however, a bit of a cut-up in my class, and when he and Luscious got to "ranking" one another, there was no stopping them for the duration of their show.

"Wasn't that a hooker I saw you with last Saturday night?" Luscious asked, starting the game.

"No, you saw me with yo mama."

"Ooooo!" the class sighed.

"All right, fellas," I'd say. "Let's be nice."

Luscious would nod his head, an enigmatic smile on his face. It told me he was thinking up the perfect rank, but he knew to wait. His opportunity would come.

It came some months later when two things happened. First, I had discovered Harold was not only a football playing fool, but also quite an artist. He could render the human form with tremendous accuracy and grace, and he did so in the margins of all my assignments and on the backs of many of his essays. His shading of forms made his subjects so three-dimensional you felt you could almost reach out and touch them and they would indeed be real. Once his secret was out, I decided to use him shamelessly.

The second thing that happened was *The Old Man and the Sea*. I wanted to get the classes fired up for the novel which at times drags even for me. Sort of like I imagine fishing itself might be. At any rate, I got Harold to draw a mural on my largest bulletin board illustrating the events on page 94. He protested when I first asked, but he came the next day armed with an encyclopedia on fish and an anatomy book. He took this assignment seriously and worked on it for days during lunch and after school before spring football practices. He did a great job. I sensed he was flattered I had asked him to take on this assignment, but I also think he wanted the rest of the world to see he was much more than just a dumb jock.

His Santiago was drawn with great precision and care. He had a dark tan, he was muscular, and he was sitting in his tattered skiff as the great marlin he had hooked broke the surface of the sea. Santiago's face bore a look of desperation. It was a strained face, bearing the deep wrinkles of age and what a hard life had inspired in him. The great fish struggled gloriously for all of us to see.

On the day we were to start the book, Harold unveiled his masterpiece from behind the brown butcher paper we had hidden it under. Many of the students were very impressed with the quality of the drawing. I even allowed a few to get out of their seats so that they could look at it more closely and admire his craft.

"Wow! This is great!"

"Whoa, who drew that picture?"

"Must have been a professional artist."

"I've never seen student work that was as competently done," the art teacher said when she came by after hearing rumors of the wonderful mural.

Every time I spoke his name, as being the artist, I could see Harold puff up just a little bit. He derived a great deal of pride and satisfaction from the praise his efforts drew. Luscious was, however, understandably jealous and was lying in wait.

After a little bit of time passed Luscious said loudly in Harold's direction, "You call that a drawing? That scribble-scrabble stuff over there?"

"I do," I said when I realized what Luscious was getting ready to do.

"Well, what kind of Neanderthal would be hulking around in the ocean like that? A person that size would sink the boat."

"I think the figure is rendered very proportionally," I said.

"And look at this." Luscious got up and went over to the drawing and began pointing out slips of the pen. "What's this foolishness? What kind of artist would do this? A third grader? Like what did you do with your crayons, man?"

Harold just smiled. The many possible retorts that he might have been formulating in his mind, stayed there. He wasn't going to give Luscious the satisfaction of a comeback. Art was too important to Harold, and he was obviously a great talent. No amount of "dissing" from anyone was going to convince the class otherwise.

Eventually, Luscious sat down.

MAY

LESSON 39

What happens to a dream deferred?
Does it dry up like a raisin in the sun?
Or fester like a sore—
And then run?

Does it stink like rotten meat?
Or crust and sugar over—like a syrupy sweet?

Maybe it just sags like a heavy load.

Or does it explode?

"Harlem"
Langston Hughes

"Pregnant? Did you say pregnant?" I asked Arthina, the biggest gossip in my sixth-period class. Her piece of news hit me like a kick to the stomach as I passed by her desk on my way to my post in the hall. I could hardly breathe.

"With twins," she said almost gleefully. "You couldn't tell?"

"No, I couldn't, and I make it a policy never to ask anyone if she is pregnant. I got into major trouble when I asked my third-grade teacher if she were going to have a baby, and believe me. I'll never do that again," I answered.

"Well, it's all over school. Marvelette is due sometime in August."

A cloud of sorrow passed over me, but I didn't want it to show when Marvelette arrived in class, so as I went through the door, I tried to think of something else. It didn't work.

Marvelette was one of my favorite students in all of my classes, especially after she endeared herself to me when I cried in front of the class over Tamara. In my mind, I can still feel her big and tender hug press in on me whenever I need a little emotional boost. She was also quite smart and, unlike some of her peers, she never forced her considerable knowledge out into the open where it might shame someone. Ever so quietly, she did her work and produced some very insightful writing. She also had an infectious laugh that made me smile almost every time I heard it. I loved her gentleness.

Marvelette really belonged in an honors class, but she didn't want to go into one. At first, I thought maybe she didn't want to work that hard. Then I suspected it was because she wanted to be the big fish in a little pond, but as the semester progressed, I could see she wasn't that prideful. Since she had no aspirations to go to college, unless it was a business college or school, she didn't need to be working in college prep classes. She was a prize-winning BCE student, and I could easily imagine her someday as the CEO of a large corporation.

But now she had come up pregnant, and pregnant with twins no less. I was crushed. I wondered how she must feel. I was afraid it would be so easy for her—a teenage mother—to waste away in some HUD apartment, all her talents and brilliance lost to a world that needs strong, successful black people.

She soon came around the corner of the crowded hall, and now that I looked at her soft ample form, I wondered how I could not have known her secret. She walked that pregnant waddle which was made all the more pronounced by the stack of books she carried. Her stomach was very definitely protruding, and I thought I saw a trace of solemnity lining her soft mocha features.

"Good morning, Marvelette," I said trying to sound as friendly as I knew how.

"Hi, Mrs. Webster," she said as she passed me and went to her seat. There she painfully dropped into her seat with a groan. I took a deep breath for her and then went back to my station.

The bell rang and the class broke into groups to finish the work they had started on Monday for a week-long project they were to present today. The assignment had been for each group to analyze and then teach a famous poem of one poet. Since we had just finished an arduous study of British writers, I allowed the groups to pick "favorite" writers regardless of nationality.

Within the few minutes after all groups were allowed to finalize their projects, the presenter from Group 1 was in front of the class making a "just adequate" presentation. Mario's report was the typical standard read-from-the-notes kind of presentation on James Weldon Johnson's "Creation." He covered Johnson's life story and how he was from Jacksonville and how they had named a school after him, etc., etc. He then read the poem in a soft, flat little voice we had to strain to hear. It was just enough to get the group a passing grade.

When the first presenter went back to his seat, Marvelette got up slowly and moved to the front of the class to make the presentation for her group. She was stunningly beautiful, I thought, as she stood before us. I wondered if the other students could see it. Her skin and hair were radiant and her clothes—made of a green, yellow and orange Kente cloth—flowed smoothly around her form.

"I guess by now all of you know about my predicament," she said, as she tenderly patted her stomach.

I realized that there was a considerable difference between the reaction to unwed pregnancy in the black community as compared to that in white society. Just a scant twenty years before, a white girl would have been sent off into exile in the night had she found herself in "a family way." She'd have to live out her term with an aunt or sister and then be forced to give the baby away to strangers. Then, just ten years ago, a pregnant teen could get an abortion. Unwed pregnancy in the white community was to be avoided at all costs because the social stigma it caused far exceeded the pain of labor or raising a "love child."

Since I cannot speak of how things were for black girls twenty years ago or even ten years ago, I can say there seems to be a kinder treatment of pregnant girls than the white society would allow. Here Marvelette was very publicly acknowledging her situation, and no one gave her the least bit of grief about it.

"Some would call this a mistake. Some would call it a problem. But I'm looking at these babies as a challenge. Something to make me stronger. After all, no one said it was going to be easy."

"Go tell it like it is, Girl," someone from the back of the room said.

Marvelette then began to read Langston Hughes's "Harlem" in a rich, silky voice. The rise and fall of her voice was appropriately paced. The reading was most powerful, especially since we could see she was using her own experience to get his message across.

When she finished reading the poem aloud, she said, "When first I read this poem, I saw my future if I let life's problems and setbacks get in my way. But I will not be denied."

"Amen, Sister," a voice called out.

"I mean, I have to ask myself, 'What is my dream?' I have thought about this a lot lately, and I have concluded that my dream is to be a real person who has lived a real life. And when I come to the end of my days and go to the Pearly Gates, St. Peter is going to know I was genuine. I was real. I lived a real existence. A hard one, perhaps, but a human life to be sure."

"Amen! Amen!" someone in the back cried.

"And I won't run from pain and sorrow. That's part of a real life. I'm going to jump right in and be alive, and sometimes it's going to hurt."

"Amen, Sister."

"It's going to hurt a lot."

"Don't you know it!"

"But that is my dream. To live a full existence. And to be the best mama I can possibly be and to give my twin boys all I can!"

"Glory to Jesus!"

"And I am going to be there for them the way my mama was for me!"

"Hallelujah!"

"She didn't need no fancy cars to be a good mama!"

"Oh, no, she didn't!"

"And she didn't need no big house."

"Glory and Amen!"

"She just needed us to love her the way she loved us. And she will guide me now."

"You know she will!"

"I am not alone in this. And I have God on my side too."

"Go, Girl!"

"I will not let my dream die and fester up and infect me with poison the way some people might!"

"Oh, no!"

"And I'm going to make things happen for me and my sons. And my dream will not be 'a raisin in the sun,' all shriveled up. No."

"Oh, heavens no!"

"And it will be a celebration of living!"

"Amen!"

"And it will not 'stink like meat.' It will sing with possibilities. And if it explodes, it will be like fireworks—a glory to behold!"

The room broke into loud applause and voices could still be heard over the din.

"Amen, Sister! Amen!"

"Hallelujah!"

I was almost speechless. I felt like I had just been to church. I was very moved by the occasion as Marvelette took a stiff bow and then took her seat.

"Humdrum" and "ho-hum" doesn't even begin to describe the performances of the next two presenters. I was relieved when the bell finally rang and the students began to move out of the room. "Marvelette," I said as she started to walk out of the door. "Yours was a wonderful speech. I am very impressed, not only with your delivery, but with what you had to say. It was quite profound."

"Thank you, Mrs. Webster. I hope I'm up to the challenge."

"With God's help," I said. "How will you handle twins, though?"

She smiled politely, as if she'd been asked that question a thousand times and said, "With twice the energy as I will with one." Then her wonderful laugh filled the air, and I smiled.

Despite her brave front, I felt that she didn't have a clue as to how hard her life was now going to be for her. I hadn't even had children of my own yet, and I could hardly imagine what rigors motherhood had in store for me. Marvelette's brave, noble words mean one thing before the children are born, but they might not seem so true when 2 a.m. feedings are keeping her awake and exhausted from all the jobs she will have to take to support these "fatherless" children.

But, then I remembered her comforting hug. Her maternal instincts might indeed make her able to rise to the challenge ahead of her. Maybe her dreams when tested against the realities of the life would stand firm, and she would only have to "postpone" them for just a little while.

LESSON 40

Somewhere over the rainbow, blue birds fly.
Birds fly over the rainbow, why then oh why can't I?
from *The Wizard of Oz*
"Somewhere Over The Rainbow"
E. Y. Harburg

The school year was starting to wind down. I could tell because we were inundated with tests that had to be given—state assessments, writing assessments, standardized tests and district tests. I was a little overwhelmed with it all, as were my students, but I finally had gotten the testing procedure down rather well. I could pass out booklets, answer sheets, scratch paper and pencils in record time. Compared with my beginning of the year homeroom fiasco, I was much improved.

On the third day of testing, just after I had given directions and set the students to their task, I heard a faint knock at the door. I tiptoed to it and opened it, only to find my friend Martha standing there in tears.

"May I talk to you?" she choked out.

"Martha?" I stepped just beyond the threshold, but stayed positioned so I could still proctor the test. "What is it?" I whispered.

"I've just got to talk to someone."

"Of course," I said, frantically signaling the hall monitor, Mr. Harrington, to come and take over the testing situation. When he arrived and agreed to cover for me, Martha and I walked down the hall to the library and to the small, deserted computer room where we could talk in private.

When we were finally situated, I said, "All right. What happened?"

"You just won't believe it. It's Dorothy Washington. I just don't know what I am going to do." Martha broke down in uncontrollable sobs, and I could only think to pat her on the back.

I only knew of Dorothy, never having taught her myself, but we teachers were all aware of her and her problems. Dorothy had been in a special remedial program at Dunbar and had probably been in remedial programs all her life. She was a nondescript child with a sweet face and smile. She couldn't read, however. No matter what any teacher could do, reading was something she just couldn't master. One day she would know the words in the passage, and everyone would celebrate. Then, the next day they could give her the same passage and she would act as if they'd given her hieroglyphics to read.

Every day she would come to the after-school remedial session, and every day they would start from the beginning. Of course, we all could see there was something going on here.

Dorothy undoubtedly had some kind of learning disability, something beyond our ability to fix. Why else would she work so hard to achieve nothing? Why else would the letters seem to rearrange themselves on the paper?

"I've worked so hard with Dorothy this year, and God knows how hard she's tried," Martha said, when she had composed herself enough to speak. I pulled a tissue from my pocket, and she gratefully accepted it.

"I've literally prayed this would be Dorothy's year. That this time she'd pass the minimum level test, and this time she'd move on out of here.

"The counselors were hopeful as well. But who are we kidding? Dorothy is borderline retarded, although they keep using the term 'special.' And because we didn't want to say the 'R' word, she didn't qualify for special education because her I.Q. was too high. Can you believe that? But she's just not able to compete in regular classes either, because her I.Q. is too low.

"My heart has been broken watching her struggle all this year as she has in the past. It was even more heartbreaking because she was over aged and had just this year to get herself back on the 'regular' track so she could graduate. But there is just no way it is ever going to happen, damn it!"

Here Martha started to sob again, and I started patting her again on the shoulder.

Soon she raised her head again to speak. "You know, once I had to help Dorothy write an essay on what would be the first thing she would buy if she had won the lottery. I think it was an assignment for home economics. Anyway, I asked her what the first thing would be that she'd buy. And you know what she said?"

"No," I answered.

"A whole box of cookies she could eat all by herself and that she didn't have to share with anybody else. Oreos.

"Well, I almost died right there on the spot. It was such a simple, Dorothy-type request. And then I got to thinking of all those spring evenings when I'd sit on the porch and pig out on those Girl Scout Mint Cookies. It was wonderful, I have to admit. It wasn't a lot to ask out of life either. And it struck me how unfair life is. There but by the grace of God . . . It saddened me Dorothy had never known such cookie joy."

"Martha, you can't be responsible for the inequities of life. Dorothy's situation is not your fault. Besides, you are doing the only thing you can that can really help her, and that is teach her. And you do it in a friendly, loving way. Why, I'd put money on it you are the high point of her day."

"But I haven't told you the worst part," Martha said, clouding up again.

"There's more?"

"Today, when it came time for her to take the final, final test—the absolutely last administration of her competency test—the one that will get her out of this program and into the mainstream where she wants to be, Dorothy pulls out of her purse the tiniest pair of reading glasses I have ever seen. They were obviously for a three-or four-year-old, and it was the first time I had any inkling Dorothy wore glasses at all. I watched her struggling to get the thick lenses on her head.

"I said, 'Dorothy, I didn't know you wore glasses.' And do you know what she said?"

"I have no idea."

"She said, 'Oh, Mrs. Williams, I be shame-faced to wear 'em most times.' Dear God in Heaven! The child can't even see the words! No wonder she could never learn to read! And I didn't know! I just plain didn't know!"

Martha was inconsolable. She wept for a considerable time until I finally got close enough to hold her in my arms. She shook terribly with sobs, and I felt her despair flow right out and into me. There are too many Dorothy's, those who slip past us—those who need more than we can possibly provide. And I started crying too; crying softly with Martha for all the children we lose.

LESSON 41

Do not go gentle into that good night.
Rage, rage against the dying of the light.

"Do Not Go Gentle Into That Good Night"
Dylan Thomas

Sometimes I think I must go through life wearing blinders.
What is obvious to most people is not so obvious to me. So when something dramatic takes place, I rarely see it coming, and I quite frequently feel like the fool when everyone marvels at my confusion.

When Rochelle took ill, I just figured it was the flu. Doesn't everybody get the flu at least once each year? I thought. When she was hospitalized, I was somewhat surprised. When I learned that it was because of her AIDS, I couldn't believe it. Not Rochelle. Not that lively, volatile mass of humanity. She was too mean to get sick like that. And that was when the obviousness of her situation struck me. How could it not be Rochelle? She was not going to go "gentle." She was going to "rage" against this thing, and I had mistaken her anger as mad about being female, mad at being in a minority, mad about not having her mother.

"Do you think Rochelle is at a stage where remission is possible?" I asked Marion Parker, the guidance counselor, who knew more about Rochelle's case than anyone else.

"Anything is possible," the counselor told me, "but Rochelle is going on two years with this disease. She is a real fighter, but I am afraid there won't be too many more remissions for Rochelle."

A chill spread over me as the thought of Rochelle actually dying became clear to me. How could I have missed this? I thought angrily. I knew I had a student with AIDS. Hadn't the dean told me so? I knew Rochelle was wasting away before my eyes. I just kept thinking her gauntness was just a function of her poor, teenager diet. Now, she was going to die, and all those wonderful poems inside her were going to be lost to the world. And even though I would "lose" her whether she had this disease or not, I felt a real grief welling up inside me.

"Is it permissible for you to tell me how she got AIDS?" I asked.

"Does it matter?" Mrs. Parker asked.

"No, I just wanted to know how this awful thing came to be. That's all."

"Transfusion. When she went through a windshield in the accident that almost killed her when she was very little, she needed many transfusions just to keep her alive. Now, one of those transfusions is going to kill her. "

"Why was I not told all this before now?"

"The privacy laws."

"Well, that doesn't really make any sense. I would have been cool about it. Besides, maybe I could have made things easier for her, or been more of a comfort to her."

"You were a great comfort to her, Mrs. Webster. You were Rochelle's favorite teacher. She told me this often."

Tears suddenly burned my eyes. "Please don't tell me that."

"Well, you were. You and your little poetry society were a

real gift to her. It was a place where she could shine and feel productive. It gave her a real sense of purpose. Now, you just hush, baby," she said offering me a Kleenex to wipe away the tears that spread down my cheeks and neck. "You have a few classes yet to go, don't you?"

"Do you think the family would object if I went to see her in the hospital?"

"Of course not. Rochelle could use some company right now. She's in St. Vincent's Hospice on Beach Boulevard. Room 214."

"A hospice? She's in a hospice?"

"The disease is going on two years."

My tears really began to roll. I wanted desperately to cave into the sobs building like thunderstorms inside me, but I had only fifteen minutes until my next class. I had to postpone my outburst until a better time. I took three very deep breaths, then I stood up to leave.

"Mrs. Webster, you're a tender-hearted soul. I can see that," Mrs. Parker said, before I opened the door to her office to leave, "but Rochelle is not going to want to see you crying. She feels a tremendous guilt already about leaving her family and hurting those who love her. She doesn't need to think she's hurting you too. You're going to have to compose yourself in her presence, at least, or your visit will do more harm than good. You don't want that, do you?"

"No," I said, taking yet another deep breath. "I can assure you I will not be an added burden to the child."

I planned my visit with Rochelle for the next afternoon. I needed time to absorb the news and to decide how I could best handle the sorrow without dragging her any deeper into despair. I called her father and arranged for an appropriate time to come. He sounded grateful over the phone. He also sounded whipped. Such life events have to be incredibly draining.

I was fortunate in that I didn't have to do much that day in the way of teaching. Testing was in full swing and all I needed to do was proctor the county standardized tests that morning. During the afternoon classes, I had the students work on crossword puzzles because they were too tired and distracted to learn much of anything literary. I was grateful for the time I had to let my thoughts wander.

I came to the end of the day with a kind of dread. I was not used to talking to dying people. Who actually is, though? I asked myself. I would merely have to go to Rochelle with an openness and honesty. I would bring her poetry. That was it. I'd bring her what gifts only I could give. I located an anthology of American poets in the library; one with all the great black poets in it.

When the time came, I drove over to the hospice, tucked the book under my arm, and bravely marched inside the building. I took a deep breath when I arrived at my destination and knocked at the door of room 214.

When the door opened, the tired face of a large black man met me.

"Hello," I whispered, "I'm Donna Webster. We met last year at Open House."

From the darkened room a small voice called to me. "Is that you, Mrs. Webster? Come on in."

The door was opened wider, and the black man slipped out behind me. I moved further into the room as two black women, one old, one just getting there, stood and came to greet me.

"I'm Rochelle's aunt," the younger of the women said. "It is so kind of you to come."

"Well, Rochelle is one of my favorite students."

"This is my mother and Rochelle's grandmother," she said as the older woman came and shook my hand. Rochelle's poem, "Neena's Bein' Place," came to my mind. This must be the very Neena.

"It is so nice to see you," the old woman said softly. "You are all Rochelle talks about."

A lump twisted in my throat, but I kept it under control.

"Well, I bet you and Rochelle have a lot to talk about," the younger woman said. "Mother and I will go and get some coffee while you two talk."

I pulled a chair closer to the bed and sat down. Rochelle looked awful. She was hooked up to all manner of tubes and wires, and the machinery was clicking and buzzing and humming all over the place. She was dwarfed by it all. Her shrunken body was almost a gray color. She looked like she was a hundred years old.

But then she smiled at me, and I could see it was the same bantam hen personality I had come to love.

"I thought you'd never come."

"I wouldn't have missed coming for anything," I said. "It was just two days ago I learned you were here."

"Bring me anything?"

"Just a book of poems. I've marked my favorites."

I handed the book to her and instantly I could tell that she was so weak she couldn't even hold it. So I took it back from her and opened it to read.

"'The Bean Eaters' by Gwendolyn Brooks . . . ." I started.

I then proceeded to read Gwendolyn Brooks poems, Maya Angelou poems, Paul Lawrence Dunbar poems, and Langston Hughes poems. I even stuck in an Emily Dickinson or two and one Robert Frost for good measure. Rochelle just closed her eyes and smiled all through my readings.

Time went by so pleasantly that I was unaware of how late it was getting to be. A nurse came in to administer medication and change the I.V., so I thought I had best be going.

"Not yet," she protested. "Not until you've read my death poem."

The nurse looked at me, and I looked at her. "I'll come back in ten minutes," she said.

Slowly, painfully, Rochelle pulled a folded piece of paper from her bed clothes.

"Here, you read it out loud for me."

I took the paper with trembling fingers and unfolded it. A tiny haiku was printed in the middle of the page.

Dying
By Rochelle Freeman
Night comes too quickly.
I shall not see another day.
Goodbye, sweet, sweet Earth.

After I read the poem with my steadiest, calmest voice, she asked me, "Well, what do you think?"

I cleared my throat and carefully said, "I think that it is the loveliest poem I have ever read in my life."

"Really? Better than Shakespeare?"

"Better than Shakespeare or Keats or Brooks or even Dickinson," I said, looking into Rochelle's still sparkling eyes. "May I keep this copy?"

"I wrote it just for you."

"I will treasure this always."

And then the nurse came back in. "Time to go," the nurse said to me firmly.

"I'll see you later," I said to the sleepy Rochelle.

"Yeah, later," she whispered and reclosed her eyes.

I gave her a hug that she could hardly return and turned to leave the room. Her family waited outside the door. They knew what I felt better than I knew what they felt. So when the aunt came over and hugged me around the neck, I had to give in to the tears. Together, we wept softly in the corridor.

Rochelle lingered for another 24 hours and slipped into a coma for another 48 hours. She died one week shy of her seventeenth birthday.

JUNE

LESSON 42

The woods are lovely, dark, and deep,
And I have promises to keep
And miles to go before I sleep,
And miles to go before I sleep.

"Stopping by Woods on a Snowy Evening"
Robert Frost

I had tried everything to stay awake. Cokes and coffee—and I had even done all of my stretching exercises more than once. Still, it was all I could do to keep my eyelids up and my brain functioning. Michael had gone to bed hours before, and Humphrey lay snoring across the stacks of graded and ungraded papers I had carefully arranged on the dining room table where I worked. It would take another hour for me to finish the last of the essay exams, and I would need about an hour to average the grades and record them on the bubble sheets for the computer. As I tried to uncross my tired eyes, I silently vowed I would never again give an essay as a final exam as long as I taught.

Under normal circumstances, I would have abandoned these

tasks to the planning period of the next day, but the next day was the last day of school for the students. I had to get all the grades done before a 9:00 a.m. deadline. I then had to monitor an awards assembly before I had to hurry downtown for a commencement practice at 12:00. The ceremony would be that night and I had to be there as well.

For some strange reason, I was given the responsibility of getting hyper, out-of-their-mind seniors into straight lines for their graduation ceremony. Like many decisions made in schools, the logic baffled me. Since I was a new teacher, I didn't know many seniors; just the ones in my two classes. Still I knew in my heart that I could handle the job. I was far more confident now than I had been on that first day of school back in the cruelest of Septembers. By this time of the school year, I felt like I had seen and done it all.

But whether I was up to the challenge of harnessing seniors with the jitters the next day was unimportant. I had pressing and numerous tasks at hand. I needed to focus my attention on the immediate present. Unfortunately, it was becoming apparent that I was going to have to stay up all night. It was inevitable.

Just then, I surrendered to a great yawn.

"Oh, this will never do," I said to myself.

I got up from my chair and went into the kitchen to pour myself yet another cup of coffee. "Maybe," I said muttering to myself, "I should try to sleep for a few hours. That might help me concentrate better."

As I sipped the hot liquid I had just poured into my cup, I reasoned that I would need a minimum of three hours sleep to be even the least bit effective. That would put me at 4:30 a.m., a mere fifteen minutes before I usually got up.

"No," I thought, "I'd better just hunker down and forget about sleeping altogether. I can sleep all summer."

At the thought of the word "summer," I was immediately refreshed. It was as if a gentle breeze had just rolled in off the ocean and touched my soul. The sound of imaginary waves filled me as a bright, imaginary sun warmed my winter-white skin. I could almost hear the gulls and see the surfers. The taste of fresh peaches came suddenly to my tongue and imaginary barbecue sauce ran down my chin.

As if kissed by some reviving god, I knew I could finish the essays and all the averaging I had yet to do, because there was a seemingly endless number of days of vacation coming my way. I could stay up all night, knowing my sweet reward for all my hard work waited just hours away. I could even stomach Thomas's misinterpretation of Hamlet's "To be or not to be" speech as being a "celebration of life," and Joshua's notion that "life was like lollipops and pickles" when you read *The Bell Jar*. Summer was going to be such a blessed joy. Even so, I met the end of this year with a tiny bit of sorrow.

I had really had a very successful first year teaching. Sure, I had had my terrible moments that year. Tamara's angry face floated across my memory and I shook my head to move her along out of my mind. Then Rochelle's wasted form came to my mind and a flood of sorrow sprang from the pit of my stomach. Tears stung my eyes briefly before I moved to more pleasant thoughts. The Wednesday Poetry Club . . . Leanne's great scholarship success . . . Percy's redemption by making a solid and honestly earned "B" on his penance test for *A Tale of Two Cities*.

I was actually going to miss the many smiling, gentle faces who had given me so much more than their respect and attention. I'd miss the power of Yasmina's poetry. The sound of Luscious telling one of his famous family stories would become mere echoes in my ears. Mark would "live forever in my heart" just as the Dickinson poem and his daffodils would. And so would the religious debates I had endured with Robert.

Each memory of a face or a smile or a moment reminded me of all the lessons that had been taught this year. There were the ones I taught as well as the ones I learned. The lessons I taught, I would file alphabetically in metal cabinets, and the lessons I learned I would tuck neatly in some corner of my heart, ready to remember and use every time I need to remember what is good and most meaningful about life—the children.

"I could reminisce all night, if I don't get on with it," I said as I filled my coffee cup to the brim and moved back out to my academic chores awaiting me on the dining table.

"Okay, Humphrey," I said as I gently moved the old, purring tabby off the last batch of papers. "It's time to finish this."

I picked up my green marker and started grading once again. I had so many more papers to go.

LESSON 43

Someone was punching me, but I was reluctant to take my eyes from the people below us and from the image of Atticus's lonely walk down the aisle.

"Miss Jean Louise?"

I looked around. They were all standing. All around us in the balcony on the opposite wall, the Negroes were getting to their feet. Reverend Sykes's voice was as distant as Judge Taylor's:

"Miss Jean Louise, stand up. Your father's passing."

To Kill A Mockingbird
Harper Lee

I don't know what prompted Lydia to say what she did when we were sitting in the teachers' lounge that final day for the kids. Maybe it was the pensive look upon my face; one that was tired from four weeks of faking smiles, after Rochelle's death, and teaching when I didn't really feel like it. Or maybe it was the fact that I'd been up all night grading papers and averaging grades.

"If there is anything I have learned from my many years of

teaching," Lydia mused, "it is that teachers get their rewards in small, almost tiny increments."

"Really?" I replied, mostly to be polite.

"And even then, one has to be very patient."

We both laughed.

"I'm trying to be patient," I said. "It's just that there are times when I wonder if I am getting through at all. When I look out there and I see heads down on the desk or blank vacant stares, I think, 'What am I doing here?'"

The image of poor Mr. Smythe suddenly came to mind—and the day of his breakdown, when he could no longer distinguish the real from the unreal.

"We teachers rarely get to see the fruits of our labors. School years pass so quickly, and the kids are out the door before we know it. I guess that's why I call teaching a 'leap of faith profession.' You just have to believe you've planted a positive seed of some kind; and even though you're not the one who will get to see it grow, you have to believe it WILL grow."

I nodded. "I guess so."

"Sometimes," she continued, "I feel like I haven't made the slightest difference at all. Then, years later, in the grocery store or at the K-Mart, a stranger will come up to me and go on and on about how I touched him so deeply or I was there when she needed me the most. Some have even told me I have made all the difference in their lives. And I'm looking into this face desperately trying to remember a name and seeing just a tiny glimmer of the kid he or she once was. That's the reward. It's that moment when all the grief and foolishness disappear, and I know I had something to do with that person's making it in this world. That's when I know I have made the right choice with my life."

I loved Lydia. Her words had been a great comfort to me all this long year. Even though I had never personally observed her math class, I had no doubt that she made the numbers make sense. She was such a great person, she couldn't help but be a great teacher.

A bell rang signaling the beginning of the awards assembly,

and together she and I made our way through the throng of happy, excited teenagers to the gym to take our stations with the students in the stands. After about fifteen minutes of crowd control and removing students from the aisles where they loved to clog up the flow of traffic, the assembly was quiet enough to say the Pledge of Allegiance and have a short devotional.

I guess we teachers and students were all tired and antsy by that time of day—that time of year. I wasn't paying much attention to what was being said. The public address system was crackly and frequently ringing with feedback. The hour dragged on and on and I spent the bulk of my time shushing the fidgeting students in my area of the bleachers.

Toward the end, when I was sure I'd scream if this didn't hurry up and end soon, everyone near me started clapping me on the back and urging me down the bleachers to receive an award.

"What?" I kept saying over and over. "Me? Are you sure? Me?"

"You won the Nicest New Teacher Award," Juanita, from first period, said to me, her face beaming.

"Is this a joke?" I asked.

When I could tell that all the eyes in the gym were riveted on me, I realized that it wasn't.

"Go on, girl!" Juanita urged.

"Go get your prize!" another voice spoke nearby. I turned to see Luscious, who grinned, but for once was not making jokes.

In my typically graceless manner, I bumbled my way through all the kids, down the bleachers, and I all but tripped as I crossed the shiny gym floor to the podium. Sparse, but sincere, applause greeted my ears. I realized that only about 200 people out of the 2,000 in there actually knew who I was. I was totally out of breath when I arrived at my destination. My cheeks burned with an unknown emotion. Whatever it was, my heart pounded and my chest was so tight, I could hardly draw breath.

When I reached the podium, I could see student awardees up on a dais. Percy, Leanne, and Tyrone were among many who were on their feet clapping and cheering loudly. Mr. Ward smiled at me for the first time in the whole year, and I was struck by the beauty and warmth of his weathered brown face.

"Congratulations!" he said, shaking my hand vigorously. He handed me a small winged statuette with the words "Nicest New Teacher" engraved upon it.

I stared stupidly at the shimmering statue in my hand. I could hardly make my throat work.

When the clapping stopped I croaked into the microphone, "Thank you."

I took a deep breath, and then words came to me almost without any conscious thought. I spoke from the depths of my heart. "This award would not have been possible without the kindness and cooperativeness of many fine young people whom we honor here today as well. To ALL the students in ALL my classes, I say, 'Thank you very much for making this first year so satisfying.' And, if it isn't inappropriate, I would most especially like to dedicate this award to two of my students who are not here today, but who are most surely here in our hearts. Andrew Barnum and Rochelle Freeman."

There was a loud eruption of applause from everyone as my words died against the gym walls. I then turned stiffly, bowed awkwardly and went back to my seat, a surge of wonder making me feel as if I were floating on air.

As I stumbled my way back up to my seat in the bleachers, I could just see Lydia's beaming face out of the corner of my eye. She mouthed the words, "See? What'd I tell you?"

I smiled back at her and nodded. "You are right!" I mouthed in her direction.

Maybe I would give this profession a chance after all.

The End

ENDNOTES

Lesson 1 Eliot, T. S. *The Waste Land*. *The Norton Anthology of American Literature, Volume 2*. Ed. Nina Baym, et al. New York: Norton, 1989. 1278.

Lesson 2 *Beowulf*. *England in Literature, Classic Edition*. Ed. John Pfordresher, et al. Glenview, Illinois: Scott, Foresman and Company, 1988. 19.

Lesson 3 Truth, Sojourner. "Ain't I a Woman?" *The United States in Literature, Classic Edition*. Ed. James E. Miller, et al. Glenview, Illinois: Scott, Foresman and Company, 1991. 270.

Lesson 4 Hawthorne, Nathaniel. *The Scarlet Letter*. New York: Bantam Books, Inc. 1981. 185.

Lesson 5 Poe, Edgar Allan. "The Raven." *The United States in Literature, Classic Edition*. Ed. James E. Miller, et al. Glenview, Illinois: Scott, Foresman and Company, 1991. 167.

Lesson 6 Thoreau, Henry David. *Walden. The Norton Anthology of American Literature, Volume 1.* Ed. Nina Baym, et al. New York: Norton, 1989. 1638.

Lesson 7 Dunbar, Paul Lawrence. "Sympathy." *The United States in Literature, Classic Edition.* Ed. James E. Miller, et al. Glenview, Illinois: Scott, Foresman and Company, 1991. 393.

Lesson 8 Whitman, Walt. "I Hear America Singing." *The United States in Literature, Classic Edition.* Ed. James E. Miller, et al. Glenview, Illinois: Scott, Foresman and Company, 1991. 296.

Lesson 9 Chaucer, Geoffrey. *Chaucer's Poetry: An Anthology for Modern Readers.* Ed. E. T. Donaldson. New York: The Ronald Press Company. 1958. 127.

Lesson 10 Kipling, Rudyard. "If—." *England in Literature, Classic Edition.* Ed. John Pfordresher, et al. Glenview, Illinois: Scott, Foresman and Company, 1988. 731.

Lesson 11 Dickinson, Emily. "The Bustle in the House." *The Complete Works of Emily Dickinson.* Ed. Thomas H. Johnson, Boston: Little, Brown and Company, 1960. 489.

Lesson 12 Shelley, Mary. *Frankenstein.* New York: Bantam Books, Inc. 1981. 61.

Lesson 13 Walker, Margaret. "Lineage." *Literature and Integrated Studies.* Senior Consultant, Alan Purves et al. Glenview: Scott, Foresman. 1997. 411.

Lesson 14 Bronte, Charlotte. *Jane Eyre.* New York: Random House: 1943. 132.

Lesson 15 Housman, A. E. "To an Athlete Dying Young." *Elements of Literature, Fifth Course.* Ed. Kathleen Daniel et al. Austin: Holt, Rinehart and Winston, 2000. 865.

Lesson 16 Capote, Truman. "A Christmas Memory." *Perrine's Literature: Structure, Sound and Sense.* Ed. Thomas R. Arp. Fort Worth: Harcourt Brace College Publishers. 1998. 282.

Lesson 17 Longfellow, Henry Wadsworth. "A Psalm of Life." *Elements of Literature, Fifth Course.* Ed. Kathleen Daniel et al. Austin: Holt, Rinehart and Winston, 2000. 150.

Lesson 18 *The Holy Bible: Authorized King James Version.* John 11:35. Cleveland: World Publishing Company. 133.

Lesson 19 Eliot, T.S. "The Hollow Men." *England in Literature, Classic Edition.* Ed. John Pfordresher, et al. Glenview, Illinois: Scott, Foresman and Company, 1988. 834.

Lesson 20 Shakespeare, William. *The Tragedy of Hamlet: Prince of Denmark.* Evanston: McDougal Littell. 1997. 9.

Lesson 21 Warriner, John E. *English Composition and Grammar. Third Course.* Orlando: Harcourt Brace Jovanovich, Publishers, 1988. 510.

Lesson 22 Angelou, Maya. *I Know Why the Caged Bird Sings.* New York: Bantam Books Inc. 1993. 113.

Lesson 23 Coleridge, Samuel Taylor. *The Rime of the Ancient Mariner. England Literature, Classic Edition.* Ed. John Pfordresher, et al. Glenview, Illinois: Scott, Foresman and Company, 1988. 466.

Lesson 24 Paine, Thomas. "American Crisis." *The United States in Literature, Classic Edition.* Ed. James E. Miller, et al. Glenview, Illinois: Scott, Foresman and Company, 1991. 98.

Lesson 25 Gibson, William. *The Miracle Worker.* New York: Alfred Knopf. 1976. 123.

Lesson 26 Orwell, George. *1984.* Evanston: McDougal Littell. 1998. 5.

Lesson 27 Wilder, Thornton. *Our Town. Traditions in Literature, Classic Edition.* Ed. Helen McDonnell. et al. Glenview: Scott, Foresman and Company. 1991. 208.

Lesson 28 Knowles, John. *A Separate Peace.* Toronto: Bantam Books, Inc. 1982. 52.

Lesson 29 Handel, George F. "Hallelujah Chorus." *Messiah.* London: Novello & Company Limited. 1992.

Lesson 30 Wright, Richard. *Native Son.* New York: Perennial Library. 1987. 66.

Lesson 31 Fitzgerald, F. Scott. *The Great Gatsby.* Collier Books/ Macmillan Publishing Company.1992. 41.

Lesson 32 Shakespeare, William. *Macbeth.* Evanston: McDougal Littell. 1997. 17.

Lesson 33 Shakespeare, William. "Sonnet 18." *England Literature, Classic Edition.* Ed. John Pfordresher, et al. Glenview, Illinois: Scott, Foresman and Company, 1988. 186.

Lesson 34 Crane, Stephen. *The Red Badge of Courage. The United States in Literature, Classic Edition.* Ed. James E. Miller, et al. Glenview, Illinois: Scott, Foresman and Company, 1991. 796.

Lesson 35 Hurston, Zora Neale. *Their Eyes Were Watching God.* New York: Perennial Library/Harper & Row Publishers. 1990. 151.

Lesson 36 Morrison, Toni. *The Bluest Eye.* New York: A Plume Book. 1994. 139.

Lesson 37 Marquez, Gabriel Garcia. "A Very Old Man with Enormous Wings." *Collected Stories.* Translated by Gregory Rebassa. New York: Harper & Row. 1984. 203.

Lesson 38 Hemingway, Ernest. *The Old Man and the Sea.* New York: Charles Scribner's Sons. 1980. 94.

Lesson 39 Hughes, Langston. "Harlem." *The United States in Literature, Classic Edition.* Ed. James E. Miller, et al. Glenview, Illinois: Scott, Foresman and Company, 1991. 796.

Lesson 40 Harburg, E. Y. "Somewhere Over the Rainbow." Metro-Goldwin Mayer Inc. 1938.

Lesson 41 Thomas, Dylan. "Do Not Go Gentle Into that Good Night." *England Literature, Classic Edition.* Ed. John Pfordresher, et al. Glenview, Illinois: Scott, Foresman and Company, 1988. 871.

Lesson 42 Frost, Robert. "Stopping by Woods on a Snowy Evening." *The United States in Literature, Classic Edition.* Ed. James E. Miller, et al. Glenview, Illinois: Scott, Foresman and Company, 1991. 512.

Lesson 43 Lee, Harper. *To Kill a Mockingbird.* New York: Warner Books. 1982. 211.

Made in the USA
Lexington, KY
04 January 2011